JUNE JENSON
AND THE
COINS OF CASSIDY
(BOOK TWO)

I0616978

EMILY HARPER

JUNE JENSON AND THE COINS OF CASSIDY

Copyright © 2017 by Emily Harper

All rights reserved.

This book is a work of fiction. Names, characters, places, and incidents either are products of the author's imagination or are used fictitiously. Any resemblance to actual persons, living or dead, events, or locales is entirely coincidental.

ISBN-13 9780994896452

June Jenson and the Shield of Quell

"Emily Harper has a very distinctive writing style and all of her books have something in common—they contain a lot of laugh-out-loud moments, feisty, opinionated and loveable heroines and a fast-paced action filled storyline."
—Cosmochicklitan

"This is a hugely action-packed book and it's all kinds of ridiculous, in the best sense… my favourite of her novels so far." *—Reviewed the Book*

"June Jenson and the Shield of Quell is a fun story that will have you hooked from page one, with some very lovable quirky main characters and lots of intrigue." *—Alba in Bookland*

White Lies

"With humour, romance and a great story that flowed flawlessly this is a debut not to be missed." *—Mrs Mommy Booknerd*

"Anyone who reads this is sure to have a smile on their face as they turn (or swipe) the final page." *—Best Chick Lit*

"It's a book I could easily see becoming a fun summer movie, filled with lots of fantastic shoes." *—Readers' Favorite Reviews*

"White Lies is the ultimate in wonderful chick-lit." *—Susan's Book Bag*

Checking Inn

"A tragicomic novel about lies, deception and colour-coded pens." *−She Loves to Read*

'It really was chick-lit at its best… that kept me gripped from start to finish." *−Make My Day Book Club*

"Emily Harper does a fantastic job of creating this quirky character who you can't help but laugh at and root for all at the same time." *−Readers' Favorite Reviews*

"Its quirkiness, well thought-out endearing characters and the backdrop of an Inn drew me in straight away." *−Cosmochicklitan*

My Sort-of, Kind-of Hero

'It has this feel-good heart-warming touch that will leave you grinning like a toon… Emily is quickly becoming one of my favourite Chick Lit authors, with fresh stories and lovable characters." *−Addictive ChickLit*

"If you are a fan of romantic and funny chick lit, check out Emily Harper's book. I can tell that this is an author that approaches life and love with a little bit of fantasy and a whole lot of humour." *−The Page Girls*

"It is a chick lit with a difference." *−The Book Corner*

For my brother, Luke, who was the first person to introduce me to the world of make believe. Oh, and bonus points for making me watch Columbo.

ACKNOWLEDGMENTS

I first and foremost have to thank my good friends and fellow writers, Dan and Linda. Your encouragement and suggestions helped me find my way with this novel, and I am very grateful to you for it. To my editor, Emily Ferko, I'd be lost without you. And to my family, who are always willing to help in any way they can, thank you.

Chapter One

"Where does this one go?" Griffin peers over the side of the box at me.

"Er—" I look down at the piece of paper in my hand and squint. "I think storage."

"Storage?" Griffin frowns and peers inside the box, causing his floppy brown hair to fall across his forehead. "It has all my toiletries!"

"Right, that must be a six, not an eight," I say, looking down at the list again through dark rimmed glasses. "Box twenty-six is the bathroom."

"Can I not just look in the boxes and figure it out? This is taking forever!" he complains. His eyes look helpless and between that and his dishevelled hair, it's difficult for me to stay irritated with him.

Difficult, but not impossible.

"No, or the whole number system will be for nothing!"

Honestly, he's been a pain in my side all day.

Griffin mumbles under his breath as he walks past me to the staircase. I manage to catch: "Already bloody waste of time", and I actively choose to ignore it.

Compromise. That's what all great relationships thrive

on—or so I'm told. The truth is, being in a loving relationship isn't as easy as I thought it was going to be, especially when your significant other drives you up the wall most of the time. I mean he tries—bless him, he *really* tries—and I should appreciate the effort and not focus on the fact he makes a right mess of things. It's something I'm working on. To be honest, the main problem might be that neither of us have a clue what we're doing. We are the wrong side of thirty and this is the first real relationship either of us has ever been in.

"June, look what I've just found!" The Professor comes out of his study with his woolly vest neatly buttoned for a change and holds up a long pair of needle nose pliers.

"Er—wonderful," I volunteer, and return to study my list. I don't know why I keep looking at it; it's a complete mess. I can't make out anything that is written for a combination of reasons: one being the Professor spilled his tea all over it, and the other being Griffin has the worst handwriting I've ever seen. My eidetic memory would have been able to memorize it if he hadn't insisted on writing it all out himself. Another "helpful" effort.

"I think I'll label them," the Professor says, his light blue eyes magnified by his rimless spectacles. He glances at the scattered boxes in the front entry. "Where's my bloody label maker?"

"Professor, I thought we agreed you were going to cut back on the labelling?"

"I have cut back! I'm only labelling the important things," the Professor argues.

"They're pliers," I say. "We have another three pairs in the shed!"

"But these are the ones that I used to get the Monopoly boot out of your nose," he says. "Don't want to forget that."

I look at the dirty pliers in his hand, covered in rust.

He's been doing well lately, much better days than I could have hoped for, especially in this later stage of Alzheimer's. The medication is working just as it should, but he's still slipping away from me. It's gradual, which is both a blessing and a curse. Before, we would have good days and bad days. It was very black and white. Now, everything seems to be grey. The days go by smoothly, he forgets things here and there, and the episodes where he can't remember who he is are not quite as dramatic as they once were. But he does forget things. Little things that seem of no significance: where his coat is, or if he turned a light off. They all seem insignificant, but everyday some new little thing is added to the list and the tally is getting long.

"Right, what about number thirty-three?" Griffin says, picking up a box from beside my foot.

"Umm…" I squint at the paper but I can't see any thirty-three anywhere. "That's for the… er… bedroom."

Griffin narrows his eyes at me but doesn't say anything as he goes back up the stairs.

"The label maker?" the Professor asks me.

"Oh, right, well… it's umm…" I push my unruly chin length brown hair away from my face and tuck the curling strands behind my ear while I look around at the foyer for the tiny blue machine. Amidst all the boxes it's hard to make out where anything is. "It should be around here somewhere."

"Absolute mess," the Professor says, shaking his head. "I've only seen that lad wear two shirts. Where did all his bloody stuff come from?"

I look around and wonder myself. There is no way all of this stuff used to fit into Griffin's bedroom. I roll up the sleeves of my oversized jumper and open the lid of the box closest to me.

"Ha! I caught you!" Griffin yells from the top of the staircase. The heel of his boot slips on the edge of the step, and he slips down a few steps before he grabs the railing to right himself. "Finally admitting defeat on your chart, I see."

"What is *this* doing here?" I say, reaching into the box and pulling out a purple floral lampshade. "This is from your Mum's sitting room!"

"Is it?" Griffin says, but I see the guilty look on his face before he's able to hide it.

I pull back the lid more and my eyes widen. "This is her soup ladle!"

"What? How did that get in there?" he asks, grabbing it from my hand and placing it back in the box. "Must have just got mixed up with all the commotion of packing."

4

Ignoring him, I walk over to another box and lift the lid. "She's packed you her microwave!"

I push that box aside and lift the lid of the next one.

"Why did your mother pack up her Barbara Streisand CDs?" I narrow my eyes at Griffin.

"It's probably just a misunderstanding. You know Mum, she's a bit flighty," Griffin says, picking up the box. "I'll get them out of the way until we can sort it all out."

"Just put it back in the car," I put my hands on my hips. "We can just drive it back over to her house."

"Right, of course," Griffin says, but doesn't make a move for the doorway. "You know, maybe I will just put them in storage for now and once we get more settled I'll take them back to her."

"It's okay, I have to nip out in a minute," I argue. "I'll drop them off for her."

I try and take the box out of Griffin's hands, but he holds on tight.

"You don't have to do that," he says.

"Yes, I think I do," I say.

"Honestly, it's only a couple of CDs," he argues.

"Is it though?" I ask, stepping away from the box to open another by his feet. "Oh look! Her dressing gown and slippers!"

I pick them up out of the box and hold them up for Griffin to see.

"Right, you know, there might have been something I've

been meaning to tell you…" he starts.

"Which is?"

"Well, you know how Mum took it when I finally told her I was moving out," Griffin says. "She was a bit upset."

"She cried for three weeks and is now on Xanax," I correct him.

"Exactly, the poor thing," Griffin drops the box and sidles up a bit closer to me.

I look to the Professor, who stands with his lips pursed. He's not Ruth's biggest fan. At first he was able to tolerate her, but then two weeks ago she took his label maker without asking and all hell broke loose.

Of course the Professor says he remembers none of it: the shouting, the ridiculing of the curlers. He even had a go at her scones.

I'd swear on my last dying breath he remembers every word.

"I told her I would visit her, that she wouldn't even notice I was gone." Griffin puts his hands on my arms as though trying to calm me down. "And, of course, she's over the moon she has you to fuss over now as well."

I will my face to remain neutral.

"She was a right mess last week when she was packing all of my stuff up—you should have seen her—absolutely inconsolable."

"Get to the point about the CDs," I say through gritted teeth.

"Well she was packing up my stuff when she—er—*we* remembered she hadn't been on holiday for a while."

I raise one eyebrow.

"So I thought it would be nice for her to take a bit of time for herself and get away from it all," he smiles.

"So why is her stuff here?" I ask. "It's not like she's moving."

"Right, she's not moving. I want you to keep that thought foremost in your mind," he says.

"Griffin," I say slowly, trying to keep my pulse steady. "Where is your mother going on holiday?"

"Well, she can't fly because of her knees," he says. "And the buses are out because of that, too. She can't go on the train because she says there's too many knife crimes on them."

"No, absolutely not," I shake my head.

"Where is she going?" the Professor interjects, still holding his pliers.

"Your mother is not staying here!" I practically yell, and watch Griffin's face fall.

"Why not? It will only be for a few weeks. A month, tops," he argues.

"No! Absolutely not," I'm still shaking my head. "What's the point of you moving out if your mother is just going to move in here with you?"

"First of all, she's not *moving* in here with me. She's coming to stay as my *guest*. I am allowed to have guests, am

I not?"

"Not ones that are still trying to nurse you," I say, picking the box back up off of the floor.

"It's not as if it's forever," Griffin says, following me as I walk to the doorway. "It's only until her nerves calm down."

"Her nerves are never going to calm down!" I say, shaking my head at him. "She just uses them to keep her hold on you."

"That is completely unfair!" Griffin says, putting his arm across the doorway to stop me from leaving.

"Really?" I raise my eyebrows. "So if your Mum is just coming for a visit, why does she need the entire contents of her house?"

He looks at the boxes and frowns slightly. "This stuff reminds her of my dad. She likes to have them around her so she doesn't forget him."

"We got her that microwave for Christmas. How does that remind her of your dad?" I ask.

"What if I tell her she can only stay for a week?" he suggests. "She just wants to help out while I get really stuck in with the screenplay."

I briefly close my eyes.

Griffin's play, which he'd been working on for the good part of a decade, was a huge success. I think the person most surprised with this result was Griffin considering he'd called off the production about ten times before opening night, thinking it was all rubbish. The reviews came in and they were glowing. Critics asked when they could see more of his work. After a year with sold out shows, a producer approached him and offered him a deal to turn it into a screenplay. It should have been fantastic news, but Griffin came home from the meeting in a cold sweat. And so began the anxiety: how was he ever going to repeat the play's success in film format. It's been nearly six months since they signed the deal and he's written nothing. Did I mention the first draft was due two weeks ago?

Honestly, I want to be supportive about this. I am *desperately* trying to be supportive. But it's all too much right now. Between moving in together, his mother's constant hovering, and the Professor labelling the entire contents of our house, I am not sure how much more of this I can take.

I may not be an expert on men—Griffin being my first real boyfriend and my best friend Charles accusing me of stealing the Shield of Quell to save his own skin—but I do not think this is normal male behaviour.

"Griffin, if your mother steps across that threshold she will never leave!"

"You are being unreasonable," he says and looks to the Professor for help. The Professor offers up nothing, and still looks shocked at the idea of Ruth staying here.

"How am I being unreasonable? For not wanting my boyfriend's mother to come and live with me?" I ask, pushing my glasses further up the bridge of my nose while balancing the box with my hip.

"She's not living with us, it's a *holiday*," Griffin argues. "And plus, I don't really see what the big deal is."

I look at the Professor, who stares back at me with wide eyes. It's very subtle, but I see him frantically shaking his head at me.

"How could this not be a big deal?" I say to Griffin.

I will myself to stay calm and try and see this from his point of view, but the more I look at Ruth's dressing gown poking out of the box, the more I want to throw all of her stuff onto the front lawn.

"We're moving in here with the Professor," Griffin says. "So what's the difference if we also live with my Mum for a bit?"

"Oh good God, it is *so* not the same thing!"

"How is it not?"

"Because, the Professor isn't well. I can't just *not* take care of him," I say this slowly to try and make him understand.

"Mum's not well either," Griffin says, trying a new tactic.

I open my mouth to argue, but then close it. I just don't know what to say anymore. Sometimes it feels so hopeless, and I have no idea how we got here. How *I* got here.

I have spent my entire adult life trying to get out of the shadow of my grandfather and the accusations of him stealing a relic from his dig site at Sutton Hoo. I thought once he was proven innocent, I would be free. Free from the whispers, free from the limitations in my work, free to live my life the way I want to live it. And really none of those things have happened.

Of course there were apologies all around, but the truth is you can never erase what has been done. We are no longer cast as the family who stole a priceless relic; now we are the family that was accused and exonerated of the crime. The page in history isn't wiped clean, and it never will be. The whispering has somewhat died away, but it was replaced with reporters hounding us for interviews, begging us for our side of the story. Our faces were plastered over the tabloids for months, and reporters still show up unannounced for a comment. What they don't seem to understand is: we don't want to talk about the scandal; we only want to talk about the history. How can I move forward when all anyone wants to do is look back?

I continue to teach Introductory to Ancient Artefacts at Oxford, but I want to discover new history– I want to have an adventure that is my own. I've applied to multiple excavation sites– not even for the lead archaeologist position. I am willing to work any position. And every time I have been denied. I know Oxford isn't happy with the articles in the tabloids. They've made me do numerous interviews and press tours on behalf of the university in an attempt to repair their image, but never seem to be happy with the outcome. Somewhere it's always written that they didn't believe us, or they might have been involved with the cover up. And somehow I get blamed for it—very discreetly of course. *It's not the right kind of publicity*, or so I've overheard. A month ago I asked the university to submit my name to a site, as they've done for countless Professors and Assistants, and they came back and offered me a guest lecture tour in some little town in Russia instead. They just want me out of their bloody hair, but can't fire me because of the negative publicity it would cause. Somehow they've managed to think of themselves as the victim in all of this when they were the ones who falsely accused my grandfather and exiled him to a life of early retirement.

And the bloody tabloids don't help. At first they were very supportive of our family and how we'd been wronged, and made Oxford out to be the pompous monsters. Then the story became old and they started hounding us for an exclusive interview. It's very difficult to repeatedly tell someone to sod off while hoping they don't turn on you for it. A reporter from the Daily Journal, Simon Locke, would wait for me to leave the house, to try and approach the Professor. He'd corner him in the shops when Griffin and I weren't looking. It started to get to the point we couldn't let the Professor out of our sights. Not that the Professor would purposefully say something wrong, it's just—well, last week he thought he was Sean Connery, so who knows what he's likely to say.

So, the tabloids turned on me, the bastards. I mean, I know I really shouldn't expect a lot from the people who try to get the latest shot of an actress without her top on, but for a moment it was nice to feel like someone was finally on my family's side. They started printing pictures of the Professor with his trousers down, speculating about how I was able to figure things out with the Shield of Quell unless I was involved in the coverup. They even tried to chalk up Griffin's involvement with the Shield as a publicity stunt to plug his play. Of course, the tabloids never come out and say anything for fear of a slander suit, but they sure are pros at insinuation.

And all it's served to do is bugger up my chances of ever having a dig site of my own. Even when I threatened to leave and take a position at another university, Oxford didn't budge. I might have been able to get away with it at first, but after the tabloids turned on me I didn't have much pull. Somehow I've gained a reputation in the archaeology community as a glory seeker, and now *no one* wants to work with me.

And then there's Griffin. I love him. I *really* do. And we aren't a normal couple—I know that. We both have responsibilities that we can't just toss aside, and for all of Ruth's faults I know that Griffin needs her just as much as she needs him. I just don't want this to be another thing in my life that has limitations.

Also, it would be nice if he didn't leave his bath towel on the floor every single morning.

"I thought you wanted to move in with me. I thought

13

we had decided that this was the next step in our relationship," I say.

"I do! Of course I do." He takes the box out of my hands and places it on the ground. "You know I want us to be together more than anything."

He wraps his arms around me and I settle against his chest.

"Please tell her she can't come," I say to him, trying not to let the desperation come through in my voice.

I need this to work out right now. I just need one thing in my life to move forward.

He kisses the top of my head and sighs.

"Okay, I'll tell her she can't stay here."

"Ruth. Not. Coming. To. Stay," the Professor says out loud as he writes in the brown leather journal he uses as a memory prompt. "The. Lad. Has. Whiskey. In. Box. Eighteen."

Griffin and I smile at each other. He brings his lips to mine, and I wrap my arms around his neck.

"Ugh hmm," a voice says from behind me.

I turn to see Dr Cooke standing on the front steps with amusement on his face.

"Nothing like young love is there, Albert?" Dr Cooke looks at the Professor, who is still holding the pliers tightly to his chest. "Perhaps that's why the great writers always try and capture it's glory."

"Hmm," the Professor idly nods in agreement.

"Though, I believe most writers find the tragedy of love to be the most compelling theme. Romeo and Juliet, Tristan and Isolde, Anthony and Cleopatra…"

I look at the Professor and frown.

"Paris and Helena, Cathy and Heathcliff–"

"Right, wonderful," I say, cutting off the Professor's list. "I think we get the idea."

"I think I read a paper on that a few weeks ago…" the Professor says, before turning and wandering back through the hallway and into his study.

"Cheery mood today, I see," Dr Cooke says and Griffin and I motion him to follow us into the Professor's study.

We find the Professor at his desk, shuffling through a stack of papers.

"I could have sworn I put it in this pile," he says looking at the stack of papers perched precariously on the edge of his desk. "Yes, I even labelled this pile as interesting material."

"Never mind about that paper, Albert," Dr Cooke says, waving the envelopes he has in his hand. "I've got much more exciting things for you to read."

The Professor's eyes light up at the sight of them, and I frown.

"What's all this about?" I ask, pointing at the envelopes.

I usually get the post myself, making sure to sift through the letters and remove the never ceasing requests from the press. I don't want him to see any of them during one his episodes and call the reporters. That bloody Simon Locke is starting to get creative, and makes the envelopes look like the Professor has won something. They *say* they want to know our side of the story, but I know better than to trust those trying to sell papers.

"These are the applications for the internship we are offering," Dr Cooke explains.

"Internship?" I ask. "What do you two need an intern for?"

They both look up at me and frown.

"My dear, we are *very* busy men. Think of all we could accomplish if we no longer have to do the mundane tasks of life," Dr Cooke reasons.

I can't help the snort that escapes. "You two spent all day yesterday labelling the jelly you made over the weekend."

"And we could have been making important discoveries if we didn't have to label those jars ourselves," the Professor argues.

"How did you even get approval for this?" I ask. "You're not even on staff at the University anymore!"

"This isn't through the University," Dr Cooke waves away my question. "Privately funded."

"Oh no," I say. "What have you two been up to?"

"Too soon to get into details, June Bug," the Professor taps the side of his nose. "Let's just say we have a lot to teach the youth of today, and the academic community is finally getting their heads out of their arses."

"Now I'm genuinely worried," I say, coming to stand

closer to the desk.

"I wouldn't mind an intern," Griffin says, sitting in the armchair. "Make my tea, do my laundry..."

"Then what would your mother do?" I snap at him before turning back to the Professor. "You realize that you would actually have to mentor this person—you can't just have your own personal slave, you know."

"June, I'm offended you think so little of us," Dr Cooke shakes his head. "We plan on teaching our new intern all we know about the world of Archaeology."

"God only knows how much time we have left," the Professor chimes in. "It would be a shame to waste the knowledge and experience that we have dedicated our lives to acquiring."

I stare at the two of them, not buying a single word of it.

"I was partial to that one," Dr Cooke holds up a peach coloured envelope. "He says he can walk a tightrope. That's bound to come in useful at some point."

"You two never leave this house!" I shake my head. "When would you need someone to tightrope walk for you?"

"Always be prepared, June Bug," the Professor mumbles as he reads the CV.

"Oh, June, this one's for you," Dr Cooke hands me a white envelope. "Found it on the floor by the post box."

I look down at the envelope and frown. It's from Oxford, and it's thick. That can't be good.

I turn the envelope over and slide my finger under the

top seal. I take the pages out, unfold them, and begin reading.

Dear Professor Jenson,

We hope that you are enjoying your summer holidays and trust that everyone is well. We are writing to inform you that this coming term we would like to offer you the position of Head of Archaeology at Oxford University. As you are aware, Dr Phillip Hurst is currently the department head, but we have had notice from the American Historical Society in the United States of America that his presence is required in Colorado at the beginning of the term on an exciting potential find involving none other than the notorious Butch Cassidy! As you may know, Dr Hurst is currently away and unreachable on a soul searching expedition in the Congo Jungle with the Nanuba tribe. We have not yet been able to reach him, but we are confident that we will be able to do so in time.

If, for some unknown reason, we are not able to contact Dr Hurst, he will continue to fulfil his position as Department Head, and in which case we would need to kindly rescind this offer. Naturally, when Dr Hurst returns from the United States you would return to your current position with Oxford University. We hope that this offer will meet with your approval and that you will find it both challenging and fulfilling to your professional development.

Regards,

William Dockery

Associate Dean

Oxford University

"The cheek!" I yell, looking up at the men in the room.

I look down at the letter again and commit it to memory, shaking my head in disgust. That's it. This is the last, final, bloody straw.

"What's wrong?" the Professor asks, frowning.

"Phillip Hurst, that's what's wrong!" I cry in outrage, crumpling the papers and flinging them into the waste basket.

"Phillip Hurst?" Griffin asks. "The bloke with the nice hair?"

I scowl in his direction.

Perfect hair. Perfect career. Perfect bloody life. He's been an archaeologist for all of five seconds. And in that five seconds (alright, eight years and two months, but who's *really* counting?) he's managed to be a part of all of these amazing excavations that have brought great press to Oxford. He's talented, wealthy (his great-great grandfather apparently invented the tea bag, so it's just salt in the wound as I love a good cup), and everything just falls into place for him in perfect order. It makes me sick, because I try *so* hard and am met with nothing but resistance, and I swear to God one time I literally saw him turn shit into gold. Well, the gold was actually just covered with some manure, but still on a camera it looked *very* impressive. He is Oxford's golden boy, and I'm the pain in their arse.

"Oxford is informing me that Dr Phillip Hurst has been offered a job in America on their recommendation," I say, looking down at the letter again.

"Why are they writing to you?" Griffin asks.

"They've offered me his position until he comes back."

"Oh, well done, June!" the Professor exclaims. "You've been after that for ages."

I look up at the men, all with eager smiles on their faces.

"They aren't really offering it to me," I argue. "They had to choose between me and Professor Stanley. Stanley is out on sabbatical while he gets his hip replaced, so surely it wasn't a tough decision. And they've made it bloody clear it's going back to Phillip when he comes back!"

"Still," Griffin shrugs. "It's something."

"It's a slap in the face is what it is," I shake my head. "I've tried so hard. I've given them my all, and this is how I'm treated."

The room stays silent, I like to think in sympathy of my plight, but most likely none of the men want to set me off.

"What's in America?" Dr Cooke asks.

"They've found something to do with Butch Cassidy and they want Phillip to run the site," I explain.

"Well, you're better off, if you ask me," the Professor nods knowingly. "No self-respecting, British archaeologist would go to the land of sex, drugs, and rock and roll for their first dig. It's too garish."

"And I've only just moved in," Griffin puts his arm around me and squeezes. "So it wouldn't be a good time for you to go right now anyways."

"And there's no room in our schedule right now," the Professor says. "We've only just got our internship approved. We have to find someone before they change their minds."

He turns to Dr Cooke and nods as they both begin to look over the CVs again, as though my problem is settled.

Settled my foot.

My nostrils flare and I try to contain my anger and keep a level head.

Well, I'm not taking the position, obviously. Let's see what they do when I tell them no and they have no one else. Then we will see who needs whom more.

I storm out of the room and walk over to the phone in the front hall, snatching the receiver off its pedestal and furiously dial the number.

"Professor Dockery's office," the small sing-song voice greets me from the other side of the line.

"Yes, this is Professor June Jenson. I need too speak with Professor Dockery, please."

I hear the gasp from the other side of the phone.

"Professor Jenson, it's me. Julia Graft!" I hear the delighted voice of recognition and quickly place it to the face of one of my bright, yet somewhat flighty, first year students. "Have you had a good summer? Mine's been great so far! My grandfather plays cards with Professor Dockery and got me this intern position, which has been amazing. Though I haven't had a lot of time to spend with my friends, which isn't to say I haven't seen them—"

Remembering Julia had a knack for talking someone's

ear off I quickly cut her off.

"Sounds lovely. Listen, Julia, is Professor Dockery there? I really need to speak with him."

"Oh no, he's gone for the day, I'm afraid," she sounds genuinely regretful. "Is there any message I could leave for him?"

I think back to all the times I heard Julia gossiping with her friends after lecture and think better of leaving the "Sod off!" message I was originally planning.

"Er—no. But please ask him to return my call as soon as he gets in tomorrow."

"Right, will do," she says. "Though it probably won't be until late tomorrow. He has a very important meeting in the morning about Professor Hurst."

"Oh he does, does he?" I say, wrapping my hand more tightly on the receiver.

"Oh yes, have you not heard the exciting news? Professor Hurst is going to be taking a term off and going to America!" Julia explains.

"I'd heard something about that, yes," I mumble.

"Professor Dockery is so excited about it. The Historical Society in the United States has even ordered a television crew to film the whole thing. Professor Hurst is going to be famous!"

Of course he is, the smug bastard.

"A television crew?" I say, as the realization sinks into my stomach. "Is the find expected to be great, then?"

"Oh yes," Julia says, and lowers her voice. "I'm not supposed to say anything, but you *are* from the same department…"

"I won't tell a soul," I say, crossing my fingers behind my back.

"Well, you know that notorious bandit Butch Cassidy? They've made a bunch of films about him—"

"Yes, I know him," I say, trying to move her along.

"Well, they think they've found some sort of lost treasure that he stole. Someone found one of the coins, I believe."

"Who? Where?" I ask, my hands now with a death grip on the receiver.

"I—" she starts and then changes her tone, "Well, hello Professor Millard. Can I help you with something?"

I wait on the line while Julia tells Professor Millard of the Philosophy Department exactly where she suspects Professor Dockery has gone for the afternoon. Judging from the information she is dishing out to everyone today, I'm very glad I didn't give her my earlier message.

I hear her say goodbye and put the receiver back to her lips.

"Professor Jenson?" she asks.

"I'm still here," I reply.

"Oh good. That was just Professor Millard looking for Professor Dockery. She said she wanted to give him some paperwork, though a little birdie recently told me that the two of them are exchanging more then paperwork, if you catch my meaning…"

"Er—wow," I say, unable to think of the right reaction to the news.

"I know, it's shocking if it's true. Can you imagine?"

"Right, well, you were telling me about the coin that was found…" I prompt her.

"Oh, yes. Well that's all I know really," she says regretfully. "I do hope they are able to contact Professor Hurst soon. Professor Dockery is so worried they won't be able to contact him in time."

"Do you know exactly where the coin was found in Colorado?" I ask her.

"It's a private home that the coin was found on. It belongs to a little old lady who owns the property," Julia says.

"Do you have their address? Or a way to contact the Historical Society?" I ask her, before I can chide myself to bite my tongue.

"Er—I'm not sure," she says, and I note the hint of suspicion in her voice and realize I might have gone too far. "Why?"

"Well… er—as a fellow archaeologist, I was just thinking if I come in contact with Professor Hurst before you are able to reach him I could pass along the message," I wait for her reaction.

"You're going to Africa, too?" she asks sceptically.

"I was considering it," I say. "I've heard such great

things from Professor Hurst about this soul trip."

"Retreat," she corrects.

"Yes, retreat, that's right."

"Well, I don't know…" she hedges. "I'm not really supposed to give out that sort of information."

My eyebrows rise, remembering all the other information I have gained from her in the last five minutes.

"Well, I just thought it would help Professor Dockery if I could even do a little preliminary research for Professor Hurst. I mean, he won't have much time when he gets back from Africa before he has to leave. But, no, if you think Professor Dockery has everything under control…"

"Well, there's no harm in a little extra research, is there?" Julia says, and I can almost envision the young girl shrugging away her concerns. "Do you have a pen?"

I quickly scrawl the number as she recites it, and log it into memory.

"So, I'll just give Professor Dockery the message?" she asks.

"Hmm?"

"That you want him to call you back. You had some sort of problem?"

"You know, don't worry about it. I don't want to add to his plate right now. I'll just figure it out myself." I say, and before ringing off I quickly add. "And better not to mention that you gave me this—I think it's just better to surprise him if my research turns up anything. We don't want to get anyone's hopes up."

"Oh yes—right," Julia says. "Probably a good idea. We'll keep it between us girls."

I hang up the phone and look down at the number. A crazy idea circulates in my head. The same thought that prompted me to get the number off of Julia in the first place. I want to stop and think about it, but instead my hand reaches for the phone again.

Ten minutes later I enter the study to find the men in the same positions I left them in, although Griffin is now slumped in the leather chair in the corner and reading CVs.

"This one types at two hundred words per minute. My screenplay could be done in…" he starts mentally counting. "Like three days!"

I walk to the centre of the room and clear my throat.

"So, I have some news," I say, stroking my finger along the edge of the desk.

"Hmm?" the Professor mumbles, not taking his eyes from his paper.

"So, it, er—turns out, I will be going to America," I say it as casually as possible.

"Hmm, good, good," the Professor murmurs and lifts another CV from the pile. "What about this one?"

"Did you hear me?" I ask, taking the paper from him. "I am doing the dig. I am going to America."

"What?" the Professor frowns. "No you're not, they've given it to that Phillip."

"Not anymore," I say, trying to suppress the giggle of excitement that is welling up inside of me. "They've given it to me, instead."

"But, how?" Griffin asks, standing up.

"They, er—changed their minds, I guess," I shrug. "They asked me instead."

"But, why?" the Professor frowns.

"Why not?" I stand up straighter. "Maybe they've finally come to their senses. I have more experience than Phillip. I'm easier to work with."

"Hasn't he done a dozen or so digs already?" Griffin asks, and I choose to ignore his question.

"And all the people at the University speak very highly of him," Dr Cooke adds.

"They've changed their minds!" I repeat. "He's out, and I'm in. I leave in three days."

"Impossible," the Professor says. "I couldn't possibly get away right now."

"Who said I was inviting you?" I turn to Dr Cooke. "You could stay with the Professor for a few weeks, couldn't you?"

"I suppose…" he shrugs, though looks hesitant.

"And Griffin, you could come to America with me," I volunteer. "They're all about films over there, it might bring you some creative inspiration for your screenplay."

And now that I've suggested it, I really warm to the idea. This could just be the chance that we need to get our relationship back on track, away from all our family obligations and hectic schedules.

Griffin thinks about it for a moment, then shakes his head.

"I don't know…" he hedges.

"June dear, I'm not sure you are thinking clearly," the Professor stands up and takes my hand. "You've never been lead on a site before. It is a very large undertaking."

"You had no problem thinking Phillip could do it," I point out, the hurt leaking through my tone.

"And do you really want your first excavation site to be in America? It's so… ostentatious. No, I think the best thing would be for us to find you a lovely little site in England," the Professor smiles at me. "It will be our new intern's first task, right Daniel?"

"Of course," Dr Cooke nods. "Only yesterday I heard of an excavation that's been commissioned in Leeds."

"Who's running that one? Gregory?" the Professor asks.

"Michael Weld, if you can believe it," Dr Cooke shakes his head. "Will be a right cock up from the get go if you ask me."

"There you go!" Griffin stands and wraps his arm around my shoulder. "The Professor will sort you out a dig. You could take the train to Leeds."

I slowly remove his arm from around my shoulder and glare at him.

"I don't need to take the train, because I will be in

America."

"June, be reasonable—" Griffin starts, but I stop him.

"Can I speak to you?" I ask, walking to the doorway. "Alone?"

He looks at the men, raises his eyebrows, and follows me into the hall.

"June, listen, I know you want to go, but I just don't think you are thinking this through. You would be going to *America!* Who would look after the Professor? What about your job?"

"The autumn term doesn't start for another three weeks. If it takes longer I'm sure they would give me a few weeks off," I rub my nose and don't contemplate that it depends on if I still have a job when they find out what I've done. "And Dr Cooke could come and stay here with the Professor. Between him and the home nurse the Professor will be fine while I'm gone."

"And what about us?" Griffin asks, and I can see he is genuinely hurt by my wanting to leave.

"Griffin, I want you to come with me," I say, taking his hand. "This will be our chance to finally have some alone time. We want a future together, but how can we do that when we are always having to look after the Professor and your Mum?"

"I just don't think—" he starts. "We can't just *leave* them. What if we brought them with us?"

"Griffin," I say, shaking my head. "I can't bring them

with me. I will be living at the site. This is my job. It's my *dream*. This is my chance to do something for *me*. How can you ask me not to go?"

Griffin rubs his hand on the back of his neck.

"Please," I plead with him, putting my hands on either side of his face. "Let's do this together."

"I—"

"Griffin?" We hear the call from outside the open front door before Ruth pops her head through the opening. "Oh, there you are. June, love, how's the move coming along?"

I lower my hands and smile in her direction. "Fine. Thanks, Ruth."

"Has—er—everything been unpacked?"

She has a very innocent tone to her voice as she peers over the edge of the boxes.

"Not quite. I didn't know you were stopping by," I say, looking to Griffin, who has an apprehensive look on his face.

"Well, Griffin forgot his wub-wub and he hasn't slept a day without it since he was born," Ruth says, coming towards me in her curlers. She holds up a ratty-old bunny who's missing an eye.

"How... er—*kind*," I say as she hands Griffin the rabbit.

"I'm just glad I was in the neighbourhood and could bring it. It's important for Griffin to feel comfortable in his new home. Did er—" she pauses. "Did the two of you get a chance to talk yet?"

"We have," I say, knowing full well what she is referring

to.

"Wonderful," she says, clapping her hands together.

"Well?" I ask, turning to him. "What's it going to be?"

"Er—" he looks from his Mum to me. He's actually sweating. Unbelievable.

"What's wrong, love?" Ruth asks, looking at Griffin with wide, innocent eyes.

"We were just talking and—" he stops, and at least has the decency to look ashamed of himself.

Well, that's it then. I have my answer. I try and push back the tears in my eyes as my throat begins to burn.

"I'm—I'm going to America," I manage to choke out and force a smile on my face. "I've invited Griffin to go, but—"

"*America?*" Ruth looks shocked and quickly looks to Griffin for reassurance.

"Don't worry, he's not coming," I say to her, continuing to smile as my lips tremble.

"I didn't say ﹣" Griffin reaches for my arm. "What I mean is, it's a big decision…"

Ruth comes to stand closer to Griffin. I look up at him and see the struggle on his face as he tries to find a way to please both of us. Ruth looks at him with tears in her eyes and I realize that I am doing exactly what I just had a go at Ruth for doing all morning. I look from him to Ruth, and I realize that this is it. This is going to be the next fifty years of my life—God knows she'll live that long just to spite me—

unless I do something about it right now.

Taking a deep breath I take a step back.

"It will be fine. It was a lot to ask, and it isn't fair to ask you to drop everything for me. I'll go to America, and you can stay here and work on your screenplay. It'll be fine," I repeat. "*We'll* be fine."

"June, wait—"

I put my hand up to stop him speaking.

"Griffin, it's okay."

I walk up the stairs to my bedroom and gently close the door.

"Does this mean you're coming home?" I can hear Ruth in the front hall.

"Mum, not now!"

Chapter Two

"Did we miss it?" I push my black-rimmed glasses up my nose as I lean on the ticket counter and strain to get breath back in my lungs.

"The gate closes in ten minutes," the lady behind the counter says. "If you hurry, you can make it."

Hurry, right. It's not like I haven't just run a marathon to get here. The alarm didn't go off this morning and I have a *very* good idea as to who sabotaged it.

"Is the other passenger with you?" she asks, peering over my shoulder. Her hair is teased high on the top of her head, and she wears just a touch too much makeup.

If I'm honest, I'm still waiting for Griffin to back out of this. I'm not really sure what he said to Ruth after I left them alone. I was sitting on our bed hugging my leather knapsack to my chest, wondering how I was going to do this without him, when he came into the room and declared he was coming to America as well. I wanted to make sure his decision wasn't guilt induced, so I told him whether he came with me or not, we would work it out. But he was adamant, and despite all of Ruth's emotional blackmail he seems genuinely excited to go (I can't prove it, but I'm pretty sure she fell down the stairs on purpose yesterday).

I think this will be good for us: Griffin and me. Our first adventure together, just the two of us. That is, if he ever makes it into the actual airport.

"He's just saying goodbye to his Mum outside," I explain, and put his suitcase on the scale.

"I need him here to check his bag," she says, pointing to the suitcase. "It's for security."

"Oh, right," I look over at the doors. "He was right behind me... Can you just put it through as my second case? I'm taking my knapsack on with me."

My trusty leather knapsack is sitting on the floor, my passport peeking out the side pocket.

"We aren't supposed to."

"What is he doing?" I look to the door again, anxious. "I *really* need to get on this flight."

"I know, we are fully booked for a week with all the summer holidays," she says sympathetically.

"Exactly," I say, trying to suppress the anxiety that is rolling through me.

This whole adventure is so unlike me. Ever since I made the decision three days ago, I've lived under a cloud of worry that someone will find out what I've done. Every time the phone rang I was convinced it was Oxford calling to tell me I was fired. Or the American Historical Society saying the jig was up. But if I ever do manage to get on this plane, I will have one whole week to figure out what I have gotten myself into before anyone from Oxford can get across the pond.

"Listen, is there any possible way to just put this bag on as my own. I really need to get out of the country."

Her eyes narrow, and I wave my hands.

"No, no, I haven't done anything illegal. It's just, I've told my boyfriend and family a little—er—*fib*." That actually might be the understatement of my lifetime. "Anyways, I *really* need to get on this plane."

She looks highly suspicious of me.

"It really isn't illegal," I repeat, not sure if I'm helping the situation or making it worse.

"Well, we really can't do anything until both parties are here," she repeats, a little more stiffly than before.

"I'm going to kill him!" I say in exasperation, looking at the door before quickly turn back to her. "Figuratively, of course."

She raises her eyebrows and says nothing.

"What could they possibly be doing?" I shake my head. "You would think they were never going to see each other again. Are all mothers and sons like this?"

I drop my knapsack on the ground in frustration.

"They're close?" she asks, and I notice a slip in her demeanour.

"If she had it her way, he'd still be on the other end of the umbilical cord," I mutter.

She pauses for a minute before nodding.

"My husband was the exact same way with his Mum,

drove me up the bloody wall."

I lean toward her in conspiratorial sympathy.

"Did it ever get better?" I ask.

"Oh, yes," she smiles, her bright red lips getting wider. "She died."

"Oh, right, well…" I say, not sure how I feel about the smile on her face.

Ruth drives me crazy, but I'm not sure I would be smiling if she'd died.

At least, I would like to think I wouldn't.

"We'll just say you have two suitcases," she says and taps the side of her nose.

"Oh! Thank you." I bend down and pick up my knapsack.

"Right, well, you better hurry. It seems you need to catch this one."

I square my shoulders and turn around in search of my emotionally stilted boyfriend. Finally he trudges through the main glass doors, wiping his eyes. His floppy brown hair has fallen over his forehead again and it makes him look younger—like a little lost boy.

"We have ten minutes to get through security," I say once he is beside me.

"Okay," he nods.

I turn around and walk towards the metal detectors. The line is miraculously short and moving very quickly.

"We should make it in time," I say, removing my shoes

and putting them in the plastic bin.

"I'm fine, by the way," Griffin quips at me.

"Griffin, she will be *alright*," I snap.

"You know, you could be a little more supportive about this, it's a big change for everyone," he argues as he takes off his belt and puts it in the bin with his shoes.

"You're right, I'm sorry," I say, shaking my head. "It's just… I'm a little stressed out about this whole thing."

"Just take one of those pills Mum gave you and you'll sleep the whole flight."

"I'm not worried about the flight," I argue. "I'm worried about what I've got myself into."

I see the frown on his face and quickly add, "Running the site."

I try to tell myself to calm down, but I honestly don't know if I will make it into the airplane before I have a heart attack. Who was I kidding? How am I ever going to pull this off? If Oxford finds out what I've done…

Oh God, I can't think about it right now. Especially with the security guard eyeing me suspiciously. It's probably all the sweat pouring from every orifice of my body that has him concerned.

"You'll be fine," Griffin assures me.

"Will I?" I try and squash the panic that is rising in my stomach. This could cost me everything: my career, my reputation. Oh God, what am I doing?

"You'll do great," he repeats, kissing my lips quickly

before being waved on.

I quickly walk through the metal detector after him and join him to collect our things off of the conveyer belt, avoiding the security guard's eyes.

"Griffin, what if I mess this whole thing up?" I ask, letting some of the panic out. "What if we get there and they figure out I don't have a clue what I am doing? I'm on my last legs with the University as it is. If I cock this whole thing up, they will fire me. I know it."

"June, you've got this," Griffin assures me, taking my hand. "You've read every book on the subject, you know more history than anyone I've met. You are going to be fine. *We* are going to be fine."

It may not seem like much in the grand scheme of things, but it's nice to know someone has faith in me. Maybe I can do this. Just get in and get out. Once Oxford sees what a smashing job I've done they probably won't even notice I've lied to everyone involved.

"Plus, if you really cock something up you can just blame it on me," he says, bringing my hand to his lips.

Just as we are about to get on the escalator I hear the start of a commotion behind me, and the panic in my body goes from worried to DEFCON One.

They've figured it out—the society must have called the University. They've come to arrest me. Or worse, fire me.

I turn and the panic is quickly replaced with confusion.

"Why should I take my bloody shoes off?" the Professor

yells at one of the security guards. "This floor looks disease ridden!"

"Albert, it's alright." Dr Cooke appears from behind the Professor. "I've brought us little booties to put on so our socks don't get soiled."

"You can't wear those," the security guard argues.

"Why in the blazes not?" Dr Cooke asks, holding the pieces of blue cloth in his hand.

"You'll have to remove your watch too," the guard says.

"I shall do no such thing!" The Professor scoffs. "I've seen that program on the telly; you lot switch them for knock offs while they go through the scanner. Read all about it in the Daily Journal."

"What is going on?" I look to Griffin, who looks even more shocked than me.

"You be careful with that! It's our equipment; it's very specialized!" the Professor yells as a man tosses a black bag into another plastic bin.

The guard peers into the bag and looks at the Professor. "They don't even manufacture those anymore."

"Exactly. It's irreplaccable!" the Professor argues.

"Sir, we have the right to look through all of your belongings and search you in the name of her Majesty's protection."

"Professor?" I ask still in shock at the sight of him.

"Oh good, June, you're here!" Dr Cooke waves to me. "Albert, she's here! No need to have her intercommed."

"Sir, please keep your trousers on!" the security guard yells.

Dr Cooke helps the Professor pull his trousers up, and they manage to make it through the metal detector with all of his clothing intact.

"Did you get a window seat?" the Professor asks me.

"What?"

"They gave me a bloody aisle seat. How can one rest when they have to constantly be on guard from having their elbows bumped by the bloody trolley?"

"Where are you going?" I ask as Dr Cooke joins us.

"To America," the Professor collects his briefcase and walks past me to Griffin. "My boy, what seat have they given you?"

"What is going on?" I ask Dr Cooke as he collects his own belongings.

"I tried to talk him out of it, June," he shakes his head. "Stubborn as an ox, that one. Though I can't say I'm not looking forward to this new adventure. I've only ever been to New York once and I have to say it was far dirtier than I had imagined. Sinatra made it seem more colourful. But the Wild West, well that's hard to pass up."

"What do you mean you're going to America?" I ask, catching up to the Professor. "I didn't invite you to come!"

"June, it's already been settled," the Professor says in a placating tone.

"Nothing has been settled! How did you even get tickets

on this flight? Griffin and I reserved the last seats."

"Oh, the organization handled everything," he waves away the question.

"What organization?" I say, the panic rising again. Who have they contacted and what have they told them?

"I told you all about this the other day. We got approved for a privately funded internship through The Association of Archaeology of Great Britain," the Professor says. "Bloody bastards tried to rescind our funding. And don't think I don't know it was that bloody Michael in Leeds trying to poach our intern! They said we needed to be involved in an actual excavation program in order to qualify for an intern of our own. Always a bloody loophole, isn't there?"

I shake my head, trying to follow what he is talking about.

"Well, I told them all about your new adventure into the foreign land and they bought it hook, line and sinker! Oh, if anyone asks, this is a top secret project commissioned by the government."

"Wait a minute! Who have you talked to about this? What have you told them?" I look to Dr Cooke to try and make sense of this, but he isn't paying me the slightest attention.

"Maybe Chester got a window seat," the Professor says, pursing his lips and looking past me. "What's holding the lad up, anyways?"

"Albert, his name is *Clint*. I've had you write it down

twice now," Dr Cooke says. "And they're inspecting his boots, I believe."

"Who's Clint?" Griffin asks from beside me.

"Our new intern! Though apparently he'll answer to anything because Albert hasn't remembered his name all morning," Dr Cooke replies. "Quite the selection process. Didn't think we would be able to narrow it down in time, did we, Albert?"

"I still fancy the bloke whose family was in the scotch business," the Professor pouts. "Think of all the birthday and Christmas presents we're missing now."

"Albert, we had to be *practical*," Dr Cooke sighs. "We're going to a foreign land and the lad didn't have a passport. And Clint is alright, you like the way he makes your tea."

"He makes your *tea*?" Griffin asks, adjusting the strap of his bag higher on his shoulder. "I need to ask my producers for an intern."

"Listen to me very carefully," I say, grabbing the front of Dr Cooke's coat. "I need to know *exactly* what you have told—whoever it is you told—about this project."

"Oh, don't get your knickers in a twist—we've barely told them anything, don't want to give the plot away," the Professor wipes his nose with his handkerchief. "All they needed to hear was America, and that you were going, and they didn't seem concerned with the particulars, did they Daniel?"

"No, they just had us sign some sort of liability waiver

and the whole thing was sorted," Dr Cooke pries my hands from the front of his coat. "And we got a smashing intern!"

"He's alright I suppose," the Professor admits. "He knows four languages; he blends into all sorts of different cultures."

"Here he comes," Dr Cooke says.

I turn around and there he is: a young freckled lad no more than twenty years old in full cowboy attire including chaps. He carries a briefcase wrapped in a dark orange snakeskin which makes his bony frame lean slightly to the right.

Right, well I would say keeping a low profile is out the window.

"Can someone please explain to me what is going on here?" I yell in frustration.

"Of course dear," Dr Cooke says. "Though perhaps we should walk and talk. I believe I've just heard the final boarding call."

The Professor hands Clint a large black bag, and Clint's knees look like they might buckle under the weight, and the panic on his face reveals he knows it.

"You see," Dr Cooke begins as we walk towards the gate. "We've had a bit of luck lately. A rather wealthy benefactor on the board of the Archaeology Association, who has admired our careers and wants to see us make up for a bit of lost time, approached us with a proposition—"

"Daniel is subtly alluding to the time that he falsely

accused me of stealing a priceless relic and the archaeology community shunned us both for close to twenty years," the Professor explains to Clint, who just nods, obviously trying to keep his focus on balancing the bags.

"Albert, I believe we have decided that was all a misunderstanding," Dr Cooke looks from the Professor to Clint. "It was all cleared up, no sense in rehashing it all."

"Daniel, we promised our protégé a firm grasp on history. We can't just skip over the parts which you don't find appealing."

"Right, should we also tell him the time you thought that common Egyptian hieroglyphic proved that Cleopatra didn't actually kill herself?" Dr Cooke argues.

"As long as you're willing to share the time you wet yourself in Prague when that garden snake went over your foot."

"We both thought it was a Viper, and you know it!" Dr Cooke snaps.

"Should I be writing this down?" Clint asks, readjusting his scrawny freckled fingers on the handle of his briefcase.

"All of you, shut up!" I yell, and people turn to look at our group. "I want to know *right now* what you are up to, or you're not getting on that plane!"

"That's what I was trying to explain before I was *rudely* interrupted," Dr Cooke fumes. "Our benefactor would like your grandfather and I to guide a young archaeologist on a excavation, hence why the funding will only be given to us if we are working on an actual site. They've given us a camera, and all we have to do is put our daily footage on the internet for them to review. They're hoping to breath new life into the world of archaeology by us mentoring a pupil in the exact art of what it actually takes to excavate a site."

"So you want to mentor Clint on *my* dig site?" I ask. "And you want to record it?"

My hands shake from the anger inside of me. I'm not sure what I am more angry about: that they have, yet again, completely taken over what was supposed to be my big break, or the fact that not only am I completely jeopardizing my career and life, but it will be recorded! What if someone on the British Archaeology Association knows and mentions this to someone from Oxford, or someone from the American Historical Society?

Oh God, this is too many organizations to keep track of… I think I am going to be sick.

"Of course we're not mentoring Clint—the lad just asked if carbon dating is something he could sign up for online. No, we're going to mentor *you*. Clint is here as our interpreter, and to send them the footage," the Professor says, walking over to the ticket counter and showing his boarding pass before walking through to enter the hangar.

"Wait, you told them you would be mentoring *me*?" My head is spinning and I feel my world slowly shrinking around me. "What did they say—did they ask you who I was commissioned under?"

That's it. I'm done. The Professor has unknowingly unravelled everything before I was even able to make it on the plane.

"They didn't really ask for specifics," the Professor shrugs. "As I said, they didn't seem too concerned with a lot of the details. Just as long as we got everything on camera and sent it back to them, I'm not sure whether they were that bothered with what we were actually excavating."

"What? That doesn't sounds right—" I start, but Dr Cooke interrupts.

"You see June, it's not about the findings, it's about the *process*. They want to see us *teaching* someone, and what those methods are. We could have dug in your backyard for all they minded."

"But we did get a lovely travelling compensation for choosing America," the Professor adds before entering the boarding tunnel.

"Wait a minute!" I say, showing my boarding pass and running to catch up to him.

"What seat have they given you?" the Professor leans over the shoulder of the women standing in front of him waiting to get on the plane.

"Listen, I appreciate that you need a site for your latest whirlwind, but I just can't bring you with me," I say to him, then turn to Dr Cooke in earnest. "Can you please talk some sense into him? This is a *very* bad idea."

"Well, I..." Dr Cooke looks away.

"June Bug, you have never been on a site before, therefore you don't have a clue what you are doing," the Professor argues. "And your American partners won't know the first thing about the preservation of sites, it's probably why they have buried treasure all over their country and they're more concerned with trying to clone dinosaurs. I don't want to see something that you have been working towards your whole life go up in smoke because you are too stubborn to ask for help."

If only he knew—

"Oh God, I've just thought!" Griffin yells, suddenly standing up straighter. "If you are all here, who's at home with Mum?"

He roots around in the pocket of his jeans.

"I've got to call her—make sure she's okay."

This is literally turning into a nightmare.

"With us at your side, you'll be back even before the autumn term starts!" Dr Cooke pats me on the back. "We know how much you love those lessons."

I look at him and weigh my options, which at this point are extremely limited. I could call this whole thing off, go home and pretend like nothing happened, but I'm kidding myself if I think these two would accept that. I'd have to tell them everything. I could make up some story to the American Historical Society and Oxford, well as far as I know they don't know anything yet, and I'm sure I could come up with some sort of explanation if need be. I could go back to my job, teach for the rest of my life and be satisfied with that. Well, sort of satisfied.

Could I live with that?

I look around at the men studying me.

"You know, if I needed your help I would have asked for it."

Which is true. I would have called if things had gotten *really* out of control.

Eventually.

"June, this is history! I refuse to let you go wandering around in a foreign land, digging up the earth and perhaps compromising a priceless relic because of your lack of knowledge; even if it is American," the Professor says.

"She must have her mobile switched off," Griffin mutters and looks around restlessly as though his mum might materialize from somewhere.

"You'll hardly even notice us," Dr Cooke tries to reassure me.

"Can I see y'alls boarding passes, please?" the stewardess asks. Judging from her accent she must be from a southern part of America.

Pretending I don't hear her, I turn to the men.

"Before we get on this plane, let me make one thing very clear: this is *my* site. I will accept your help, I will welcome your knowledge, but this is *my* site. I am choosing to let you come with me and participate in this, not the other way around. Also, I want you to promise me that you won't send any of the videos in until we are back home."

By then Oxford will know what I did and either I'll be the new golden child or I'll have been fired anyways.

I look at them, waiting for their acceptance.

"Quite reasonable," Dr Cooke shrugs.

I'll take it.

"Boarding passes, please?" the stewardess repeats herself.

"Right, Colin if you could," the Professor hands his boarding pass to Clint who manages to grasp them in his two spare fingers.

"What are you doing?" I ask him.

"June, Colin speaks American," the Professor admonishes. "Let him do his job."

"Oh for heaven's sake, I think—"

I watch as Griffin gives Clint his boarding pass and takes mine out of my hand.

"Well, don't I just have the gosh darn best news for y'all folks," the stewardess says as she flips through all the boarding passes. "We sure are booked up here, and the only seats we've got left are in our premium section. If you could just scooch on behind me, we'll get y'all tucked into your new seats and get y'all in the sky in a jiffy."

The Professor frowns at the woman, before turning to Clint.

"The airline upgraded us to first class," Clint explains.

"I'll take the window!" the Professor says, following the

stewardess.

***

Alright, I'll admit it. First class is amazing. The chairs are huge. You get served hot food with actual silverware. They've even come around and cleaned my glasses twice. I didn't think I was going to be able to eat again, but I've actually been able to get my left eye to stop twitching as I ate a lovely vegetable lasagne.

"I think we should go over some of the preliminary background work before we get there," I say over my shoulder to Dr Cooke and the Professor, who are sitting directly behind Griffin and myself.

Knowledge is power, and the more we know the better prepared we will be. And the better prepared we are, the sooner we will find the treasure and the sooner we can get the hell out of there before all hell breaks loose.

"American history," the Professor snorts before taking a sip of his third complimentary whiskey. "Never thought I'd see the day we would be going to study it, am I right, Daniel?"

"I've always thought the Americans to have a rather colourful history," Dr Cooke takes a sip of his gin and tonic, and then sees the Professor's scowl. "Very ostentatious, though."

"Can we perhaps put our prejudices aside for the time being and focus on the *history*," I argue with them.

"But that's just it, June. With the Americans, the lines

between fact and fiction are so bloody blurred who's to say what's real?"

"I believe that argument could be made for all of history," I point out.

"Yes, but the rest of us are more humble about it," the Professor says, draining the glass.

"Well the relic is in America so I think it's wise to make the best of the situation," I argue. "Who's to say what we might find when we get there?"

"Yes, and they do make very fine whiskey in the West, Albert," Dr Cooke reminds him.

"Moonshine," the Professor's eyes light up.

"If we could focus…" I say, "A coin has been found on a ranch in Colorado which is believed to be from a treasure buried by Butch Cassidy and The Wild Bunch Gang. After robbing a bank that was carrying the Railways money, they fled to their hideout and buried the treasure somewhere along the trail in the canyons—or at least, that's what the rumour is."

"I love those old Western movies," Clint pipes up from across the aisle. "I used to watch them all the time when I was a boy, my mum would put them on for me. It's how I learned to speak American."

"Right, back to the task at hand," I say, getting out my notebook. I've already memorized my notes, but want to be able to add anything if the two men have any insights. "Sticking to the history books, we don't know much about the treasure, but we do know quite a bit about Butch Cassidy. His real name was Robert Leroy Parker. Born in Utah in 1866, he formed the group The Wild Bunch Gang, and they travelled the West robbing anyone they felt like. He really did it all: train robbery, bank robbery, he even stole land. He was an outlaw for years, pursued by the Pinkerton Detective Agency until he eventually fled for South America with Harry Alonzo Longabough, more commonly known as "The Sundance Kid". It's believed he was killed in South America in a shoot out, but others swear he died an old man in Utah."

Griffin lets out a low whistle.

"Those coins must be worth a pretty penny today," he says, and I watch as his eyes lose focus over the thought of the fortune.

"They've only found one coin, so far," I remind him. "It doesn't necessarily mean the rest of the coins are going to be there."

"But what if they are?" Griffin asks. "Who would keep the money?"

"Well, each country has their own laws regarding this," I say.

"If you find something in Britain, it belongs to her majesty," the Professor says. "As it rightly should. History is preserved, and the finder is given a bloody good fee for discovering it."

"In Roman times, it was divided equally," Dr Cooke says. "If a man were to find a bag of coins lying on the street, half would go to him, half to the ruling body."

"But what about America?" Griffin asks.

"I believe their motto is "finders-keepers"," I say. "There are some legal hurdles, and some treasures have been confiscated if they hold great historical value, but for the most part if you find it on your property, it's yours."

"And that is what is wrong with this bloody country," the Professor hiccoughs before leaning into the aisle. "Where's that stewardess gone? I need a refill."

"I think you've had enough," I argue, and glare at Clint, warning him not to order the Professor another drink.

"So what else do we know about the treasure?" Griffin asks, drawing my attention back. "How do they know the coin they found is even real?"

"They don't yet," I say. "They want me to authenticate it."

"Will you be able to tell if it is?" he asks me.

I nod. "I've seen enough American coins from that time to know what to look for. I've seen what the coin should look like from books, studied the bank's seal and the markings that would be on the coin. I think I'll have a pretty good idea if it is real or not."

"So, what are you going to do after you find out if it's real?" he asks me, lowering his voice so the Professor can't hear.

"Well, I'll excavate the area where it was found," I say, trying to sound confident.

"Right, and how exactly do you plan on doing that?" he asks.

"Well, I—er—" I push my glasses up the bridge of nose as I try and think for my answer. Oh god, I'm drawing a complete mental blank. That's never happened to me before. I have an eidetic memory, I can't *not* remember something even if I want to.

"You'll be fine," Griffin puts his hand on top of mine and squeezes.

All I can manage is a nod. This is not good. This is *really* not good. I close my eyes tight and try and bring the pages of the textbook to the front of my mind but instead all I see is the Professor shaking his head in disappointment.

"This is pretty exciting, actually," Griffin leans over to place a kiss on my temple. "I have a feeling I will get some great material for the screenplay from this."

"Listen, while we are in America I need you to do something for me—" I swallow convulsively. "I need you to er—keep a look out."

"What?" he asks.

"I just—I need you to keep an eye out for anything— er... *odd.*"

"Odd? What do you mean?" he studies my face and narrows his eyes. "What's going on? Why is your eye twitching like that?"

"Nothing it's just—" I swallow again and look around to make sure the others aren't listening.

I turn back to Griffin and suddenly have the urge to tell him everything I have done. To share the burden with someone else so that, perhaps, I won't be a moments notice away from a mental breakdown. I open my mouth to do just that, but then close it again.

I can't. He's the one person who actually believes in me, has *faith* that I can do this. How can I tell the one person who is so confident in my abilities that I actually lied and tricked people into giving me this opportunity?

"It's just—" I search for an explanation. "Well, it's Phillip."

"Who's Phillip?" Griffin frowns.

"Phillip, from the university," I explain.

"Oh, the bloke with the hair—"

"Yes, him," I interrupt irritably. "I was—er—warned by someone that he isn't too pleased with me taking over the site and might come trying to er—cause trouble."

"Who warned you? What kind of trouble?" Griffin sits up straighter.

"Not trouble per se," I say, trying to find a way to explain. "I just want everything to go smoothly, so I was hoping you could keep an ear out while we are there…"

Griffin nods. "Right, and just remind me why we hate this guy again?"

"Griffin!" I say, sitting further back with an annoyed look on my face. "You know perfectly well he has tried to sabotage my career every chance he gets."

"Of course," Griffin nods, though still frowns. "How exactly again?"

"Well I can't just list it all... I mean, it's a combination of things..." I sputter. "It's like my parking spot."

"Your new spot? The one the university gave you last month? The one they painted your name on so everyone knows it's reserved for you?" he asks.

"Yes. That was Phillip's spot and he got them to repaint it and give it to me," I cross my arms in bitterness.

"The nerve!" Griffin says in mock reproach.

"He got them to give me his old, repainted spot, and then he took my old parking spot," I explain.

"So you got a nice, freshly painted parking spot and he got your old spot that's missing some of the asphalt?" he shrugs.

"My old parking spot is closer to our offices and lecture halls," I say, leaning forward. "He got them to repaint his old parking spot when they were repaving that area and gave it to me so everyone would think he's the gentlemen, but now he has *my* parking spot that's closer to the campus."

"Right..." he says in a neutral tone.

"And that new course they offered me, about the hieroglyphics," I say. "Phillip got them to give me that."

"That bastard," Griffin shakes his head in outrage.

"He got them to give it to me, because once I accepted it, they announced the project with the National Geographic Society for the excavation for Tutankhamen's tomb. The

University thought my case load was too packed to work on the project, but miraculously Phillip had room on his schedule because he hadn't taken on the extra course work."

"How was he to know they would announce that?" Griffin asks. "You didn't know…"

"Oh, he knew," I say through clenched teeth. "He knows *everything*."

Griffin blinks, saying nothing.

"Don't you see, he's a manipulator! He comes off as this suave gentlemen, but all of the stuff is just for his own benefit! And I have to accept it or I will come off as an ungrateful brat."

"Are you sure he isn't just trying to be nice?" Griffin says, scratching his head. "I mean, he got you a new parking spot, he got you that course which I know was above your tenure…"

"That's what he *wants* you to think," I say, pointing my finger in his face. "But he knows *exactly* what he is doing."

"So, in Colorado… what should I be looking for? Should I watch out for people trying to give you directions? Maybe Phillip has told them to give you the longer route to get you in trouble on your expense account for the petrol," Griffin hides a smile. "Or if there's a clue hidden in a book should I tear it out and burn it? You never know if Phillip put it there to—"

"You know, what? Just forget it," I interrupt, scowling at him. "I'm sorry I asked."

"June, I'm kidding," Griffin laughs, ruffling my hair. "If you say someone is being mean to you, you just point them out. I'll make sure to get them after the bell rings."

I narrow my eyes, and lift my chin high, staring in the opposite direction

"Alright, I'm sorry," Griffin says pulling my chin so he can see my eyes. "I believe you. In a way I'm grateful you hate him. I don't like the idea of you working so closely to someone with such perfect hair."

I snort and my resolve to stay angry with him slips.

"But what's got you all worked up? Has he said something to you? Has Oxford?" Griffin looks concerned.

"No, nothing," I say, and force a smile on my face. "Just forget I mentioned it, everything will be fine."

"You wouldn't have mentioned it if it were nothing," Griffin argues.

"Honestly, it's nothing. It's just me getting stressed out over nothing again," I say, putting my hand on his arm and giving a reassuring pat. "I think I'm just letting my nerves get the better of me, worrying about nonsense."

Griffin narrows his eyes at me, as though trying to judge my statement for the level of truthfulness.

"Honestly, I shouldn't have mentioned it," I say, placing a kiss on his cheek. "You were right before, it will all be great."

He holds my gaze a little longer than necessary, then smiles.

"You will be great," he says reassuringly, then returns my kiss.

I need to calm down, take some deep breaths and try to ignore all the changes to my carefully laid plan. I just need to get some sleep and I'll wake up and everything will be fine, because this time everything is going to work out from the get-go.

"Treasure," Griffin says in a dreamy whisper.

I close my eyes and will my brain to calm down.

Chapter Three

"Un-bloody-believable," the Professor says from his seat beside me in the back of the rental car. He reaches in his breast pocket and produces a small flask.

Through my shaking, I try and find my voice to remind him about drinking with his medication.

"Give me that," Dr Cooke swipes the flask from the Professor's hand and quickly puts it to his own lips.

"I thought that went pretty well," Griffin says, making his way around the front of the car.

"You nearly bloody killed us!" Dr Cooke argues after the Professor snatches his flask back.

"It's not easy driving on the other side of the road!" Griffin says.

"Yes, and I'm not sure answering your mobile as you enter the motorway the wrong way helped that much," I snap.

"You know I've been waiting for Mum to call me back. I'm worried about her being all alone," he pauses. "Besides I got us here, didn't I?"

I look up and see Clint is still sitting in the back seat with his seat belt on. His face is drained of colour and his eyes refuse to blink.

"The important thing is we made it," I say and suddenly I feel a renewed excitement about our next adventure.

About half way into the flight I decided to nix my pessimistic outlook.

The fact is I'm here, I'm doing this, and it is going to be great.

Also, the stewardess said we were too far into the flight to turn back when I cornered her by the loos.

The view before me is stunning. Massive peaked mountains loom in the far distance, the grey stone wall broken by the white powder of snow. The lush green vegetation at the bottom covers the expansive ground below makes the scene that much more breath-taking.

The house in front of us is a small log cabin built onto the side of a large hill, the front flush with the earth, and the back supported by stilts. A small stream of smoke is puffing from the stone chimney by the back door, and the effect is too charming for words.

"America," the Professor says from beside me as he takes in the view.

"Is it as bad as you imagined?" I raise my eyebrows at him and fight a smile.

"We'll see," he says before turning back towards the car. "Clive, what are you doing in there? Get the bloody camera going!"

I tense at the mention of the camera, but then relax when Griffin walks up beside me, putting his arm around my shoulder.

"So this is the Wild West, huh?" his voice reflects the awe of the view. "I must admit, I expected it to be a bit more... *dry.*"

"From what I've read, Colorado is very lush in vegetation. It's just the canyons that are a desert."

"It's just, when you say the Wild West, you picture dusty towns with tumbleweed rolling through the main street."

"That's for the films, my boy," the Professor says, clapping Griffin on the back. He looks over his shoulder and when he sees Clint has finally got the camera going and is pointing it in his direction, he repositions his body to face it. "Colorado is one of the few states that has such diverse terrains, including farmland. The outlaw, Butch Cassidy, was a ranch owner himself. The ranch was farmed, had cattle and other livestock, though of course it was just a front for him to pursue his criminal activities."

The Professor's booming voice is a step away from shouting.

"We have now arrived at the site where this mysterious coin—believed to be a piece from the missing bounty belonging to Butch Cassidy—was found. I haven't seen it myself; haven't even been offered a bloody cup of tea though we've been here nearly five minutes. If we were in our good-mannered nation they'd have the kettle on and a biscuit in my hand already," the Professor shakes his head and gets his journal out of his pocket. "Must note the hospitality is lacking for my internet report later."

"They want you to write a report, too?" I ask, feeling the colour drain from my face.

"Just a little report to accompany my video," the Professor says.

"*We* are supposed to write a report," Dr Cooke says, pushing himself into the camera frame beside the Professor. "And *we* are supposed to appear on camera together."

"Alright, you tell them about how Butch became an outlaw in the first place," the Professor gestures to the camera.

"Can we start again? I wanted to wear my new hat," Dr Cooke says, walking over to the back of the car for his bag.

"So you've done some research yourself, then?" I ask the Professor. "I thought you didn't care for America and its history."

"I didn't know I hated caviar until I tried it, June Bug," the Professor says before walking towards Clint and the camera. "Did you get me from my left side like I told you?"

"Albert, we agreed you'd be on the right and I would be on the left because of my lazy eye," Dr Cooke says, positioning himself beside the Professor in front of the camera, this time with his black cowboy hat on. "Check your journal, I made you write it down."

"I don't recall any such—"

"Hello?" I hear the tentative call from behind me and I turn to see a small woman waving in our direction. The high arch in her back causes her to permanently lean forward, causing the wisps of hair that have escaped from her bun to fall in front of her eyes.

"Er– Hi, my name is June Jenson. I think–" I watch for a sign of recognition. "I was asked to come because of a coin that was found on your property?"

I push my glasses up the bridge of my nose and begin to doubt that we're at the right house.

Her eyes study me before a grin splits her face. "You've come!"

"I– yes. Umm… I know we are a few weeks early, you might not be expecting us–"

"I found the coin," her voice comes out almost as a giggle.

"Right," I frown in confusion. "And you are expecting someone to come and look for the rest of them?"

I look at her floral draped body; her dress has as much shape as a potato sack and I suspect she sewed it herself.

She nods in response.

"Well… that's me."

I stare at the petite woman but she doesn't move. I suddenly wonder if this whole thing is some sort of a ruse. Did the American Historical Society even confirm this woman's story?

"Come with me," she says, and turns to walk back to her

house without waiting to see if we follow.

I turn to look at the others, wondering if I am the only one who thinks this is strange.

"Bloody Americans," the Professor shakes his head, muttering.

"Is she—" Griffin points to the side of his head. "Is she all there?"

"I guess we better go and find out," I say, and start to follow her.

I need facts. I'll go in and find out what's going on before jumping to any conclusions.

Sometimes looks can look deceiving... I'm sure when the neighbours saw the Professor walking that dog last week wearing only his underpants while smoking his pipe they weren't thinking that they were looking at one of the great historians of our time. They were probably more concerned where he got the dog from.

I mean, obviously I couldn't ask the Historical Society any questions when I spoke to them, or it would have aroused suspicion about why I couldn't get the information from Oxford. Maybe the whole dig is a bit of a wild goose chase and I've risked everything by hopping on board.

Her pace slows greatly as she starts on the incline up to the front door of the house, but she never looks over her shoulder to make sure we are following her.

We reach the front door at almost the same time as her; leaving it open is her only invitation inside.

The house smells strongly of varnish and a fire burns in the corner. The logs crackle merrily, and the red and blue furniture enhance the wooden floor giving the whole home a warm, cosy feeling.

"Come, come," she waves her hand over her shoulder and she winds her way through the room past all of her furniture.

We walk into the large farm-style kitchen, a harvest table off to the right. The cabinets have no doors and the shelves are jammed full, but somewhat neatly stacked, which seems to be a theme running through this woman's house.

"Here," she points to the table, silently urging me to sit.

I can see the shape of a small coin sitting on top of a cloth. Beside the coin is a small glove, which I assume is there for handling the piece.

I lean over the table, rather than sitting, and study the coin. The patina is consistent with the late nineteenth century. I can see that someone has carefully removed the dirt from the top, but either lack of skill or knowledge has kept grime in the deeper grooves.

"Has anyone from the American Historical Society seen this?" I ask her, peering over the rim of my glasses.

"Only the pictures I sent 'em," she shrugs. "Said they couldn't get anyone out here till the beginning of next month."

"They've commissioned an entire excavation without seeing the coin in person?" the Professor asks in indignation.

"The time, the resources, and this could end up being change from someone's pocket!"

"And the timing," Dr Cooke clicks his tongue in reproach. "Countless things could happen to the area in a month, especially if the coin was found on the surface area."

"It was a good thing we were able to come, Daniel," the Professor nods. "Maybe these Americans will take note of the proper way—"

I clear my throat to get their attention.

"May I?" I raise my eyebrows.

Without waiting for her permission, I pick up the glove and put it on. I lift the coin up to the light to get a better look at the markings.

"Well?" Griffin comes to stand beside me and peers at the gold coin.

I look to him and then turn to the Professor to nod.

"I think you might have a genuine coin from the Great Railroad Robbery of 1901."

She claps her hands together once. She looks as though she never had an ounce of doubt that the coin was the real deal.

"I knew it, I just knew it."

"Chester," the Professor snaps his fingers and gestures for Clint to follow him over to me. "June, explain your findings."

I look up to see the red light of the camera blinking, the lens trained straight on my face.

"I—er—well, to begin the coin is gold," I say, holding it up for the camera. Feeling foolish for stating the obvious, I mentally shake my head and start again. "It appears to be genuine based on the weight and the colouring. Butch Cassidy was very particular about what and where he robbed. He preferred bank notes over coins for the simple reason they were less heavy to carry as he was running away from the crime. On the day of the train robbery in 1901 it was originally believed that he again only stole unmarked bank notes in the value of roughly forty thousand dollars. However, after he fled to Argentina, other members of his group were found with their share of the loot, which included many bags of gold coins. Some speculate the total was as much as thirty thousand dollars. In todays market they would fetch well over two million dollars."

I look down to the coin in my hand.

"From the mid 1800's to just before 1907 there were two gold coins in circulation. They both had the liberty head imprinted on them; one valuing a single dollar, the other five dollars. This is the five dollar coin," I hold it out for everyone to get a better look at. "You can see the female silhouette's hair is up, with two ringlets falling down. The single dollar silhouette has more hair down. And the protrusions along the edges, they equal the right amount."

"But how do you know this is one of the coins from Butch Cassidy, and not just any other coin from the time?" Griffin asks, peering over my shoulder to get a better look.

"I feel I should ask that," Dr Cooke says, trying to push his way closer into the line of the camera lens.

The Professor waves away Dr Cooke's concerns and squints his eyes at me as he waits for my response. I can't tell whether he is testing me or generally interested.

"I—" I look down at the coin, suddenly very nervous at my first test as a lead archaeologist, especially with the camera so close to my face.

Taking a deep breath, I decide to rely on my greatest strength: my eidetic memory.

"Because, this has all the markings of the coins circulating at the time of the robbery, however it also has an additional marking which makes it almost certainly one of the coins from the bank robbery. When the other members of the Wild Bunch Gang were found with their coins, the coins themselves were missing the date stamped along the bottom. Usually the coins are stamped at the royal mint, however, these coins were being transported to another facility where they would be stamped. They had not yet reached the facility when the rail car was ambushed, meaning the coins had not yet received their date stamp."

I hold the coin closer to the light to get a brighter reflection off of its surface.

"This coin has all the markings from the time, yet no date stamp. We won't be able to definitively say if this is a coin hidden by Butch Cassidy until we are able to locate the rest of the coins—it's the only way to verify that it isn't just a fluke lost coin that happens to coincide with what we know about the lost treasure. But the aging, and the coin itself, makes me inclined to hope that it very well could be."

The Professor and Dr Cooke share a knowing look between each other before the Professor turns back to me and nods.

"Well done."

It takes me a moment of standing and staring at him in silence before I am able to truly process what he has just said.

"Thank you." I smile at him as I feel Griffin's warm hand on my lower back. Between Griffin's understanding of what this means to me, and the Professor's acknowledgement of my academic ability, I'm swept into a deep fondness for both of them.

"June, don't pinch the coin like that, you're disturbing the earth. We can study that to help us determine the location of further coins," he says, turning away from me to look into the camera lens. "Once we are shown the location where the coin was found, we can study the earth and the soil on the coin itself to narrow down its movements, and determine how wide to make our digging range."

"I knew it!" the woman whispers beside me, a gleeful smile on her face.

She looks at the coin in a worshipful manner and I feel now might be the best time to question whether she understands what she is committing to before we go any further.

"Um, Ms—" I stop, realizing I don't even know this woman's name.

"Pearl," she supplies.

"Right, Ms Pearl—" Her giggle cuts me off.

"Just Pearl," she says to me, bouncing from one foot to the other.

"Okay, Pearl," I smile. "You do realize that the ownership of this coin and further findings will be subject to the courts as to who owns this treasure."

She looks at me, obviously noting my discomfort, before bursting into another fit of laughter.

"Oh, I've done my research," she says, rubbing her hands together. "Those coins are on my land."

I look around at the modest kitchen. The stove looks like it is as old as Butch Cassidy himself.

"Yes, but they were stolen from the State. Whether or not the fact that Cassidy may have buried the treasure on your property evokes the 'finders-keepers' law…"

"Spit it out girl, what are you saying?"

"What she is saying is even if we find the coins, you may not get to keep them, or sell them," the Professor sniffs, and I can tell he is uncomfortable that the motivation of this dig seems to be for the monetary value of the find. "Of course, there are other historical items that could be of great value: what the coins are buried in; perhaps documentation kept with them. The *history* this finding could potentially tell us about what happened to Cassidy after the robbery…"

"I know what I'm entitled to," she nods at me, ignoring the Professor.

"I just wanted you to be fully aware—"

"Don't you worry about me. You just worry about finding those coins," she says, nodding her head as though that is that.

"I'm going to properly document everything," I say to her. "I want to publish my findings, so there are some contracts involved that I have brought for you to sign. And they would like to film the process, so I am sure they have some forms as well…"

"Honey, you promise me you'll find those coins and I'll sign whatever the hell you want. I've already signed everything else you've sent me."

"What do you plan on doing with them?" I ask. "If we find them, that is."

"I got plans," she says, nodding her head.

I look at her, but she stares right back without flinching. I want to argue with her that the coins should really belong in a museum, but the truth is, it's not my decision what she does with them, and quite frankly, I have bigger things to worry about at the present.

"Right, well we can't do much tonight as the sun is going down, but we will be back first thing tomorrow morning and you can show us where you found the coin," I say.

"The men can go get the bags," she says, walking over to the stove and grabbing a heavy cast-iron skillet.

"The bags?" I frown.

"I'll start the corn bread," she says, pushing things around in the cupboard beside the white fridge.

"We can't bloody stay *here*," the Professor whispers to me a little too loudly.

Pearl's hands stop moving things and I quickly amend, "What the Professor *means* is we couldn't possibly impose on you—"

"No imposition," she waves away my concern. "Got it all sorted. Wasn't expecting you for a few weeks, mind. I only have the one spare room in the house, but I get the impression the two of you aren't opposed to pushing the beds together."

She looks from me to Griffin and my face burns scarlet.

"But if there's one thing my mama taught me was always be ready for guests. No, I got the bunkhouse all gussied up for guests."

"Bunkhouse?" the Professor turns to Clint.

"I think it's a sort of guest suite," Clint says, though he frowns thinking about it.

"A guest suite?" the Professor repeats as he and Dr Cooke share another look. "That should do nicely."

Chapter Four

I take a deep, calming breath and look at the valley below me; I can't imagine a more beautiful place. Wildflowers seem to have taken over the area, the grass only visible on the steep banks. The flowers are a cloud hovering over the ground, inviting someone to go and lay down amongst them. In the distance I can see the snow capped mountain peaks, the green at the bottom a direct contrast to the white tips. They must be massive up close, but from this distance I can pinch them between my fingers. The rushing water of a nearby stream makes me wonder what else you could possible ask the earth for. All you ever need is all around you sitting here.

"It's beautiful, isn't it?" I ask Griffin wistfully, and bring my coffee cup back up to my mouth.

"Mmm," he says, looking at the same view as me.

"Couldn't you just stay here forever?" I ask, putting my head on his shoulder.

"At least until the Winter," he nods in agreement.

In the distance a small deer peeks her head out of the forest, her ears perked in our direction even though we haven't made a sound. I hold my breath, even at this distance not wanting to do anything to scare her off– hoping she might come out and we can watch her find her morning meal. Her eyes blink a few times before she goes as quickly as she came.

"You know, Butch Cassidy, or Robert Leroy Parker, as he was known at the time, worked on a dairy farm similar to this. That's where he met a cattle rustler named Mike Cassidy who become somewhat of a mentor to him." I wave my hand over the grass so the blades tickle my palms. "Then he went to Wyoming and worked as a butcher and gained the nickname 'Butch'. When he became an outlaw he assumed the name Butch Cassidy in honour of his friend."

Griffin nods, though I can tell he isn't as interested in this as I am.

"What do you think Pearl's story is?" Griffin asks, plucking a blade of grass.

"I was thinking about that last night and I'm not too sure about her," I say, shaking my head. "I mean, obviously she wants to find the coins for the money, but she seems to live a modest lifestyle and enjoy it. Though where she gets her income from I'm not sure. Maybe her late husband left her something. I think she mentioned she was married once, didn't she?"

"Maybe she's one of those nutters who eats beans for every meal and will die a millionaire. Mum's Aunty Rachel did that, left half a million quid to the bloody Climate Change Protection."

"Well that was very socially conscious of her," I smile at the disgust on Griffin's face.

"That woman used an aerosol can till the day she died. She did it to thumb her nose at Mum."

"Why would she want to do that?"

"Who knows, you know how woman can get…" When my eyes narrow at him he quickly amends. "Or just people in general."

"Well, I think people have a right to leave their money to whatever they want. They earned it," I say, playing with the grass in front of me. "How was your Mum on the phone yesterday?"

Griffin sighs. "Alright, actually. She sounded a bit distracted but, bless her, she was probably trying to keep a brave face for me."

I make a sound in agreement.

"So, how do you think Pearl earns her money?" Griffin peers around. "It doesn't look like she farms anything, and I can't imagine her having a proper job."

"Maybe she's found treasure on her land before," I say, the thought popping into my head. "She was convinced if we found the treasure she'll be allowed to keep it. Maybe she knows more than she's letting on."

"Maybe you should call that Historical Society and ask them what they got her to sign," Griffin suggests, and I feel my face flush. "They've probably told her exactly what's what in that contract and she hasn't read the bloody thing properly."

"Er– yes, good idea," I say, avoiding his eyes.

"Maybe her husband did leave her money, like you said," Griffin suggests.

"Maybe," I acknowledge. "I think he died when they were much younger, though, I haven't seen pictures of any family in the house. Actually, I haven't seen any pictures at all."

"And she's a little... *odd*. I mean, we're not used to normal, but there's just something about her that is just... weird."

"You talking about my mule?"

We hear the voice from behind us and turn to see Pearl standing there with a long piece of grain sticking out the side of her mouth.

"Your..." I hedge, shooting my eyes to Griffin.

"Dolly's been grazing on the wrong field, messed her up in the head a bit," Pearl says, pointing her chin out to the field off to the left. My eyes rise in the direction and I see a mule tied to a post just beside the bunkhouse. It seems to be going in unsteady circles.

"Is it alright?" I ask as the animal bumps its head into the post it's tied to and stumbles to the side.

"She will be, just gonna take a few hours," Pearl lets out a sound this is somewhere between a snort and a giggle.

"She looks like she's on her last legs," Griffin points out as we watch the mule sort of collapse beside the post. "I think she's dying."

"She ain't dyin'," Pearls tutts. "Stupid thing's as high as a kite."

"What?" I ask, turning to Pearl.

"I told you, got in the wrong field. She knows she's supposed to stick to the one by the front of the house, but she grazed over to the other side of the valley and got into my cannabis leaves. Serves her right, I say, cost me nearly a thousand bucks before I caught her."

Griffin and I exchange wide eyed glances.

"Would of shot her dead if she weren't my best friend," the woman laughs as she shakes her head. "She won't do it again I reckon, anyhow. You come up to the house when your finished gazing at grass and I'll show you where I found the coin."

Griffin gives some sort of affirmative answer as I try and maintain my composure.

Oh my God. We are living with a drug lord.

Once she's a safe distance away, Griffin turns to me again and begins to open his mouth.

"Bloody guest suite my arse!" I hear the bellow from the bunkhouse as the door is slammed open. Poor Dolly tries to jump at the sound, but all she manages to do is kick out her legs.

The Professor puts on his hat and looks around until he spots me. He quickly walks down the steps and starts towards us.

"Not a word," I say to Griffin quickly.

"Where would I even start?" Griffin shakes his head.

Dr Cooke peaks his head out of the bunkhouse doorway before following after the Professor.

"June, she has us sleeping with the bloody livestock!" the Professor yells. I try to tell him to lower his voice but he pretends he can't hear me. "There's hay and shit everywhere!"

"Professor, I'm sure it's not that bad," I gesture for him to calm down.

"Daniel lost his reading glasses in the portable loo last night. Carl spent the better part of the evening fishing them out," he says, shaking his head.

Clint has finally appeared as well, his thin arms trying to carry all of the Professor and Dr Cooke's suitcases while keeping the camera pointed at us.

"There's not even a television in there," Dr Cooke admonishes. "We had brought a few Westerns to watch, didn't we Albert?"

"No need for television, Daniel. We got the late night special listening to two cows getting ready for the spring calf season!"

Griffin takes pity on Clint and goes over to help him with some of the bags.

"We're moving to a hotel," the Professor says firmly, before taking one more look at the bunkhouse. "In my youth... maybe. But I'm too old to use a toilet that doesn't flush."

"Right, well maybe we need to take a minute to regroup," I say to them, running my hand through my tousled hair and trying to think this through.

I'm not a prude by any means. I mean, I haven't ever actually done drugs myself, but I'm almost positive I've seen some deals done on campus. Or they were exchanging notes... it's hard to say. But the important thing is I didn't report anyone. Because I'm like that—the cool, hip, young professor.

Also, I didn't want to get the reputation of being a snitch like Professor Grath on top of everything else.

And I've read some rather remarkable papers on the medicinal qualities of cannabis, the results with epileptic studies are really quite extraordinary. Still, this little web of deception I've weaved here is complicated enough without the added bonus of digging on an illegal drug farm.

There is no way the Historical Society knows about this. Or Oxford for that matter. A part of me is kicking myself for taking this away from Phillip. God, to see his face when he learned this was a grow-op—and in front of that fancy television crew he was bringing! Well, I imagine it would look somewhat similar to the way mine looks now.

"Right, here's what we will do," I say, looking around me at the men as now both Griffin and Clint struggle with their bulky loads. "I'm going to just pop in and have a word with Pearl, then we'll go to the nearest hotel in the area."

"Well, there's no need to go right now," the Professor says, adjusting the brim of his hat. "Let's go and see where the coin was first, and then we'll go to the hotel in the afternoon for tea."

"Well, the thing is, something has come up," I say, meeting Griffin's eyes before turning back to the Professor. "And I'm not entirely sure we want all our belongings to be here."

I imagine a drug bust while we search for coins and my palms start to sweat. If Oxford sees me on the six o'clock news being put in the back of a police car...

I expect the Professor to argue but it is Dr Cooke who chimes in.

"What do you mean? What's going on?" he asks. "Is something wrong with the project? I've told all my friends we were going to be on the internet! I called my publisher about a second book deal."

"You kept that bloody quiet, didn't you?" The Professor turns to Dr Cooke. "I don't suppose you were going to ask me to co-author, were you?"

"Albert, honestly—" Dr Cooke tries to look offended, but it comes off more nervous. "Of course I was. Just didn't want to mention it until we saw what we were getting—"

"My arse you were!" the Professor yells.

"Please!" I yell at both of them to stop. "At this rate I'm not sure anyone will want their name associated with this project, so you can both pack it in!"

"What are you on about?" the Professor asks me, still glaring at Dr Cooke from the corner of his eye.

"Well, the truth is…" I look at the men staring at me, the red light from the camera blinking.

And now I realize that I don't just have my own neck on the line here, I have their necks too. They've got their internship, their reputations that they've taken so long to repair. I've lied to some of the most influential people in our field of study, and if I go down, I will now be taking these two with me. And now adding criminal charges into the mix—it's too much and it's a risk I just can't take.

There's still time. We could leave now with minimal damage done. I open my mouth to confess everything to them, but then close it when I see the Professor watching me. He was so proud of me last night. He believed it me. I'm about to shatter all of that, and to end up with nothing to show for it.

"Griffin and I have discovered a… problem," I lower my voice, hoping it won't travel to the house. "We figured out where Pearl is getting her money from. This is a cannabis farm."

"That's where they grow weed," Clint pipes up from behind the Professor.

"My boy, I know what cannabis is!" the Professor snaps.

Clint's cheeks redden and he shrinks back.

"Are you sure?" Dr Cooke asks, looking around the farm.

"She told us so herself. Dolly got into it," I say, pointing at the mule making low noises and sprawled out on the ground.

"I told you this would happen," the Professor shakes his head. "Bloody America is riddled with it. Thank goodness we didn't eat that dessert last night!"

"I highly doubt she would have drugged us," I argue.

"Did I not warn her, Daniel?" the Professor asks as though I haven't said a word.

"I might still be able to get us on the Leeds assignment," Dr Cooke mutters, rubbing his chin. "June wouldn't be lead archaeologist but they might let us have our own corner of the site... Michael will have a bloody field day with this. Cocky bastard."

My heart sinks as I see the two of them discussing the situation and how to best get us out of it. It's all my fault. And they don't even know the half of it. Even if I found the coins now, how could I go to Oxford and beg forgiveness and tell them on top of everything else I excavated a lost treasure using their name and connections on an illegal grow-op?

"The Historical Society couldn't possibly know about this," I say.

"I don't know about that," Griffin shrugs. "I mean, like the Professor says, this is America."

"What do you mean?" I ask.

"Well, things are different here, aren't they?" he says.

"I've seen more people with guns in the past day, than I have in my entire life. I think things are more... *relaxed*... here when it comes to this stuff."

"Breakfast is up!" I hear from behind me and jump when I see Pearl a few feet away, watching us with a smile. How does she move so quick and soundlessly like that?

"Er—Pearl, can I have a word?" I ask.

"Yeah, sure," she says, looking to the others for someone to speak.

"Alone, if that's alright?"

"It's your news, you tell who you like," she shrugs and turns to walk back to the house.

I offer the others a small encouraging smile and then I follow Pearl into the house. Inside the kitchen I can smell fresh bacon mixed with coffee.

"As soon as you're all finished eating I'll show you the map," Pearl says to me. "Can't go with ya, I got to be here for a visitor this afternoon."

A visitor? Is that code word for one of her dealers stopping by?

"Well, the thing is Pearl, I'm not entirely sure if I can take on this project anymore."

"What? Why the hell not?" she asks, putting her arthritic hand to her waist.

"Well, I'm not convinced my employer would be okay with me participating in this excavation."

"How come?" she prompts. "They sent you, didn't

they?"

"Well, I didn't realise—what I mean is, I didn't know that you were—that this is—" I wrack my brain for the politically correct term but I'm not sure how to go about it.

"Just spit it out girl," Pearl says in frustration.

"Well, I didn't know the land the project is commissioned on is growing illegal narcotics. The legend of Butch Cassidy is a bit sensational, to say the least, and I think there will be a lot of media attention if we were to uncover the coins. Adding drugs to the mix may be a bit much."

And the last thing I need to do is bring more questionable publicity to Oxford's doorstep.

"What does that have to do with anything?" Pearl asks, frowning. "That historical society you're working with knows all about it and they don't seem too concerned."

"They know?" I ask, but then quickly shake my head. If they know, then I technically should know as well. "We've been having a bit of trouble with our email lately. That information must have got lost in er—cyber space."

I offer her a laugh, shrugging.

"You do know it is legal to grow marijuana in Colorado, right?" she asks me.

"No, I didn't," I answer, cursing myself that the only things I read about Colorado were from tourist guidebooks.

"But as you said, not sure if your fancy university would like it too much if they found out you were working on a cannabis farm," she sighs and pats my shoulder. "Don't be too hard on yourself, we all gotta answer to somebody."

I offer her a smile and my brain starts turning. How upset would Oxford *really* be? They wouldn't be *pleased*, I'm sure, but it isn't as though they will be pleased with anything I'd done up to this point. I *could* use this as an out and the Professor and the others would never find out what I've done. Maybe the real problem I'm worried about isn't whether Oxford will forgive me, but whether the Professor will.

"Well, you gotta do what you gotta do," she says standing up straighter. "I'll just ask that society to find someone else."

"Yes, I suppose you will," I nod.

"Yeah, they were supposed to send another guy anyways, but then you showed up. If truth be told, I was glad for the sight of you. They made the other guy sound like a hoity-toity, but you ain't like that."

"He is," I mutter.

"I had other offers of course," she says, lifting up a paper with her scrawls on it. "A feller from California, and got one from Italy here. He said he could bring me some of those fine cheeses I've read about."

I open my mouth to speak again, but close it.

It changes nothing. If Oxford thought I was capable of this they would have given it to me in the first place, and I have more than my own career to think about. The Professor just recovered from the scandal of Sutton Hoo, a scandal that plagued him for over a decade. And there's Dr Cooke and Griffin; I can't do this to them.

"I'm sorry, I just can't," I say to her, and turn around and leave before I change my mind.

Back outside, I approach the waiting men with a smile plastered on my face.

"She was very understanding," I tell them.

"Good," the Professor says. "You've made the right choice, June. You have to think about your entire career and what this would do to it."

"Hmm," I nod.

He doesn't know how true his words are. They thing is: I've been buggered from the start. If I went through with this, if I discovered the coins, I would probably have lost my job, and that would crush me. I do love teaching, it's something I've wanted to do since I was a little girl. I just wanted something more as well. I wanted to become a *name* in the field. But I guess that's not life; in the real world there are few happily ever afters and you just have to work with what you've been given and find happiness in that.

I think what I am most disappointed in is myself. Because if truth be told, when it actually got down to the wire, I knew I was going to chicken out. I'm just not a big risk taker. The thing that happened with the Shield, the car chases, the fighting, the risks—I did all of that because I didn't have a choice. It all sort of got thrown at me, and the survival instincts came out. But this... I don't have to do this. This is a choice, and when it really comes down to it, I don't have the gumption to see it through.

The Professor looks off to the mountains and frowns. "It's a pity leaving the coins though; I hope someone will find them one day and preserve them properly."

"Someone will," I say. "Cannabis is legal in Colorado and the Historical Society is continuing on. They'll send someone else."

I don't mention it will be Phillip. Best to let them assume it will be someone from another university.

"What?" the Professor and Dr Cooke say in unison.

"She's had offers all morning. Someone from Italy has promised her chesses," I say, shrugging.

"We're staying!" the two of them say in unison.

"What? We can't," I argue.

"What about June's career?" Griffin asks them, frowning. "While she was inside you were both going on about how this would ruin her."

"Everything's changed my boy, try and keep up," the Professor picks his journal up off the top of the suitcases Clint is still holding. "Carl, get the camera going."

"What are you doing?" I ask them. "I– Oxford would not approve of this. I can't stay, I could be fired."

"Oh, who cares!" the Professor waves my argument off.

"You all did a minute ago!" I say.

"June, I'm only going to say this once and I will never repeat it, nor admit to it, ever again," the Professor straightens his shirt before buttoning up his jacket. "I was wrong. This is obviously the chance of a lifetime for you— for all of us. You don't waste moments like these! I can promise you they won't come around again."

"But what about Oxford?" I argue.

"Don't tell them," Dr Cooke says, searching in his bag for something. "We'll find the coins and ask for forgiveness after."

I stare at him as he repeats the same argument I've been repeating over and over in my head since we got here.

"You—you think they will?" I ask him tentatively.

"Is it really that bad?" Dr Cooke shrugs. "The woman says its legal here. They've trusted you to come here to run the site, they should trust you to make these sorts of decisions."

I shake my head and turn to Griffin, trying to plead with my eyes for him to make this hard decision for me.

"I don't know, love," he says, shaking his head. "But I'd say you need to do what's right for *you*... not anyone else." His eyes move to Dr Cooke and the Professor, who are already getting themselves ready for the camera. "Why don't you just call Oxford and ask them if it's alright?"

"I can't," I say, putting my hand to my forehead. I realize from Griffin's look that I answered too quickly.

"What?" Griffin looks at me puzzled. "Why not?"

"I—" I start, but the words don't come to me quick enough.

"They'll say no," the Professor says, adjusting his hat. "No, she's better to just go on with it. Once we find the coins they won't care where she's found it. Cannabis farm or not."

Griffin doesn't take his eyes from my face and I have to turn away to think properly.

I bite my lip, weighing it all up.

I've already accepted I will most likely get fired over this. But is it fair to put these men in jeopardy and potentially find nothing? If I tell them what I've done, they could make up their own decision. But if I don't tell them, and the time comes, I can honestly say they had no idea that they weren't involved.

It's a big risk, but I could also make the discovery of a lifetime.

You don't waste moments like these because I can promise you they won't come around again.

This is what I have been after for over a year now… Can I risk giving it up and possibly never getting another chance?

Before I can change my mind again I lift my head and yell "Pearl!"

"Here, honey," she says, standing just behind the Professor.

I really don't know how she does that.

"I've changed my mind. I want to stay," I say, and then think to add, "If that's alright with you."

She looks at me for a long moment before nodding.

"Breakfast is still hot."

"Lovely," the Professor rubs his hands together, smiling at her. "Carl, put the suitcases back in the guest suite."

I notice Griffin is studying me intently.

"What? You don't think I made the right choice?" I ask him.

"No, it's not that," he says, his eyes narrowing. "It's just... not like you."

"I know," I say, shrugging. I breathe in deeply and offer him a smile before turning to follow the others into the house.

Chapter Five

I take a deep breath in and release it, surveying the lush grass that covers the valley in front of me. It really is a remarkable sight. England is very green, of course, with all of our countryside and rain, but this landscape is so different from back home. There are so many conflicting elements here: the mountains, desert, green farmland; it's a wonder they can coexist so happily this close together. It's also nice to see and feel the sun, which only seems to hint at making an appearance back home.

"This is it," I say, nodding decisively. "It's going to be a good day."

I found my trench coat at the bottom of my suitcase and have my brown leather knapsack on, equipped with a first aid kit and granola bars. I wanted to take some water but Pearl showed me the fresh stream close by to where she found the coin.

"June, dear," Dr Cooke comes to stand behind me. "Might need to have a word with the Professor."

"Hmm?" I ask, peering over my shoulder.

My eyes widen as the Professor approaches wearing full

cowboy attire.

"What's he doing?" I ask.

"He's got a bit confused this afternoon. We were watching a few Clint Eastwood movies last night on Clint's portable computer, and he thinks he's in the Wild West. Of course, *technically* he is, so I think my arguments have just confused him more," Dr Cooke explains. "And that Clint wasn't much help, gave me a little bit of lip after breakfast because I asked him to do something while he was fiddling around with his mobile. Kids and their devices nowadays."

He shakes his head at me and I nod, but then stop suddenly. I'm young. Well *youngish*. Clint isn't that much younger than me, yet Dr Cooke is grouping me with him and the Professor. I'm not sure why, but I'm slightly offended.

"Ma'am," the Professor approaches me, lifting the brim of his hat.

Looking at his leather chaps—which look remarkably like the ones Clint was wearing at the airport—I lift my chin and turn back to the valley.

"We can do this," I say, nodding my head again and telling myself not to look back at the Professor.

Dr Cooke looks sceptical but shrugs.

"Clint, my boy, got all the gadgets?" Dr Cooke asks Clint, who has come to stand beside the Professor, a small bag slung across his chest and a plastic grocer's bag in his left hand.

"Just need a camcorder, really," he shrugs, but then at

the men's frowns he adds, "I mean, I've got the special lenses and stuff, too."

He lifts up he grocer's bag for them to see.

"Excellent," Dr Cooke clasps his hands. "And will Griffin be joining us this afternoon?"

"No, I don't think so," I say, trying to put Griffin and his never-ending suspicions out of my head. I never should have asked him to keep an eye out for anything suspicious, he keeps looking at me a funny and I can swear he's knows something is up. But how could he? And all that business this morning didn't help. The trouble is, he knows me a little too well. I think I side-stepped the whole cannabis farm problem without kicking up enough fuss, though, so instead of keeping an eye on everything else that is going on—like I asked him to—he seems to have turned his attention to me.

I know he's trying to help, but do I constantly harass him about the fact he hasn't written a bloody word for that screenplay and is likely never to finish it? No.

At least not aloud. So you'd think he could show me the same courtesy.

"So which way, little lady?" the Professor drawls, looping his thumbs through the belt loops of his jeans—jeans which are a good size too small for him. Looking at Clint's lanky frame in a pair of maroon skinny jeans I wonder what else the Professor will find in the young man's suitcase.

"Er–" I look at the map Pearl drew for me, and the compass in my hand. "That way, I think."

"Right, how far you reckon?" the Professor's southern drawl makes him actually sound sort-of American.

"About three kilometres?" I guess, studying the map. "Are you up for walking that far?"

"You can't walk that!" Pearl says from behind me, causing me to jump. "That forest you have to pass through is rough terrain, you wouldn't make it half way. I've saddled the horses for you. They've all been to the stream many times before, so they shouldn't have any trouble finding it for you."

"Horses?" I ask. "I don't think any of us know how to ride horses."

"I ride," the Professor says, lifting his hat in Pearl's direction. "Ride them, train them, breed them."

"Breed them?" I raise my eyebrows.

"I too can ride," Dr Cooke says, obviously feeling as though he is being out done by the Professor again. "Learned in prep school with bloody John Wayne here."

I turn to Clint, my last hope of support.

"I used to be in charge of the ponies at the fair," he says to Pearl. "You don't have a small one by any chance? Or maybe a really old one?"

"My horses are real gentle," she says, turning to me. "If you ain't ever ridden, I got an old bicycle in the shed."

Right, so I'll look like a plonker while everyone else is riding horseback.

"I've ridden," I lie. "I was more worried about the

Professor."

"Right, it's settled then," she says, and waves us over to the four horses she has tied up.

Where did they bloody come from? Is it me? Am I so worked up about this excavation and all the lies that I've told that my mind is on a hiatus in protest?

The Professor approaches the large white horse and mounts without hesitation. Watching him, Dr Cooke approaches the next biggest horse, and after two attempts heaves himself into the saddle as gracefully as he can muster.

Clint chooses the smallest of the four horses—the little bugger—and just has to go on his tip-toe to swing his leg over.

The last horse is not particularly big but looks a bit jittery. It keeps backing up and moving forward and rolling his eyes, where as the other three stay obediently in place.

I look at its face, making eye contact, and then quickly realize that was a mistake. I think it can sense my reluctance because it starts moving sideways, trying to get away from me as best he can while tethered.

"Oh, he'll be all right," Pearl says, smacking the horse's bum. "You just got to show him who's boss."

"Right," I say, nodding. I begin to walk over to the horse, who strains to move further away from me.

"Would you like to switch?" Dr Cooke suggests.

"No," I say quickly, seeing how large his horse is. "I'll be fine."

"Give me your foot," Ruth extends her hand for my foot. I obediently place it in and she hoists me off the ground. Crikey, that woman is strong.

"Right, now take the reins, and remember, show him who's the boss."

I nod, taking the reins from her.

The Professor is the first to set out off followed closely by Dr Cooke. Clint tries to stay balanced in his saddle with the small camera strapped across him, and the bag full of lenses sitting at the front of him.

I wait for my horse to follow the line, but he doesn't move. Adjusting the reins in my hand I flick them against the horse's neck like I've seen them do in the movies, but the bloody thing refuses to budge.

I look back to catch Pearl rolling her eyes before she smacks the horse on the backside again, causing the animal to start moving forward.

"Try not to get lost in the woods," she mumbles before turning back to the house.

Right, I can do this. I'm in the right direction, I'm moving forward. Everything is going according to plan.

"Because now *I'm* the boss," I declare loudly.

The sound startles my horse, and we are suddenly galloping past the Professor and barrelling into the forest.

I blink rapidly as my eyes adjust to the dark forest. After only a few gallops past the first trees, darkness engulfs me in a cold, eerie blanket. The trees are still—almost *too* still and a pair of white eyes stare at me. The sight is so unnerving that it causes me to shiver under my trench coat despite the muggy warmth in the air. Pushing my glasses up the bridge of my nose I hold onto the horses reins tightly and twist back in the saddle to locate the others.

Clint's brown eyes are huge as he tries to look in all directions at once, obviously terrified at what might jump out at him. Dr Cooke looks not much happier with his current surroundings, but the Professor leads his horse forward, seemingly at ease with the darkness.

"It's—er—a bit dark," I say, and am pleased to note my voice only quivers slightly.

"Reminds me of the time I stormed the Alamo," the Professor says, spitting and hitting Clint on his maroon clad legs. "We had to travel through all sorts of caves then."

"You bloody never—" Dr Cooke starts in outrage, but I quickly put up my hand for silence as a bush not too far ahead begins to rattle.

The horses seem to notice something as well, their ears pricking up at the sound. The brown palomino beneath me starts jerking forward of its own accord.

"Um… are there *rattlesnakes* in Colorado?" I whisper and take a death grip on the reins of the horse, my knuckles turning an unnatural shade of white. I quickly think of the contents inside of my knapsack and frown with the realization that unless I can tempt a snake with a granola product, my packed survival kit is clearly lacking some items.

"Yes, ma'am," the Professor says as we edge closer to the bush.

It could be my imagination, but it seems now multiple bushes are shaking and producing noises that are a mixture of hissing and rattling.

Stay calm, I warn myself. You are the leader here. Set an example.

"Right, the thing to remember is they won't attack unless they think they have reason to," I say, thinking back to all of the information I've read on snakes. "They're quite vulnerable really, with no arms or legs—"

"Can we join them in a pity party later?" Clint says in a strangled voice, his eyes wild with fright.

"Their striking distance is only as far as the length of the snake's body," I say, quickly trying to calm everyone with reason, all the while keeping my eyes on the ever-shaking bush. "If we all put our feet up—"

"Out here, due process is a bullet," the Professor says reaching into his pants, and producing something that looks like a pen.

"Oh, now you're quoting John Wayne's bloody movies!" Dr Cooke says in outrage, turning in his seat to look away from the concentrated face of the Professor. "June I will handle this!"

Dr Cooke reaches into his own bag and produces a small silver cylinder, not much bigger then a cigarette lighter. Before I am able to ask him what it is, he raises it high in the air and presses the small button on the top.

The sound is deafening as the fog horn blares through my ear drums. First stunned by the onslaught of the sudden noise, it takes me a second to realize my horse's feet have begun moving at lightning speed underneath me. My body tilts backwards in the saddle from the sudden movement.

The only thing that keeps me in the saddle is my earlier death grip on the reins. We barrel through the forest in a frenzy, and I duck my head as a low overhang branch comes up from no where in front of me. After we pass, I raise my head and think about looking back to see if the others are following, but I can barely stay in the saddle as it is, my bum bouncing so hard up and down at the unrelenting stride of the horse. I hear a distant screaming in the background that could be coming from any of the men, but the sound is close enough for me to know that they can't be far behind.

I look ahead and see a huge fallen tree blocking our path. Trying to prepare myself for the sudden stop, I adjust to sit more centre in the saddle, but the horse's ears perk up again and suddenly there is no ground beneath us. The Palomino soars over the fallen tree and the force of my bum hitting the saddle upon landing nearly throws me off completely. I see something out of the corner of my eye and turn as a large feathered creature whips past my head, knocking my glasses sideways.

What seems like hours later, but could only be minutes, the horse begins to slow its breakneck speed, and the trees around me start to thin and small beads of light penetrate the relentless darkness. We finally pass through the last overhanging branches to a bright, green clearing, and when safely in the middle, the horse turns around so I am facing the forest clearing we just emerged from. Moments later, the men file through, one by one. Clint looks like he might have died and what I'm now seeing is his ghost. White as a sheet, small jerky movements cause his body to twitch to the left, his hair standing on end on the left side and his eyes wild. His mouth is open and he keeps making noises as though he wants to say, or scream, something but it's caught in his throat.

Dr Cooke doesn't look much better himself; his hands are clamped around the rim of his hat, pulling it so low on his head he can barely see, and I wonder how long he has been holding onto it like that and how he managed to stay on the horse.

The Professor seems to be the only one not completely traumatized by the situation, and it's times like these that I am almost thankful that he is able to go into a state of unawareness. In fact, adjusting himself in the saddle with a triumphant look on his face you would think he just had a great adventure.

"We're okay," I say to myself more than anyone. "We've made it."

Clint lets out a noise than sounds a bit like a donkey, and I take it as a good sign he is able to make any sound at all.

"Actually, it wasn't all that bad really—" I say to them, but Dr Cooke raises a shaking finger.

"June, your hair," he says, his finger pointing at me. "There's something—"

"Get it off!" I shriek, letting go of the reins and putting my hands to my hair. I shake my fingers through the brown curls, screaming. I panic and fall sideways off the Palomino, still shrieking. I whip my head up and down, while trying to shake off whatever is on me.

Almost sobbing, I look up at Dr Cooke who is racing towards me.

"What is it? Is it gone?" I ask as a shiver runs down my spine at the thought of something living on me.

"It's gone, I think! It's," he scans the ground around me and visibly relaxes. "It might have been that twig." He points to the ground, and I see a small twig with a leaf sitting out of place on the lush green grass below me feet.

The adrenaline drains from my body and I slump forward.

"Friend, you better get another line of work; this one sure don't fit your pistol," the Professor comments as he gets off his horse and makes his way towards us.

"Oh for God's sake," Dr Cooke mutters under his breath and puts a hand under my arm to help me stand up.

Chapter Six

I don't know how—I *literally* have no clue—but by the grace of God we miraculously emerged from the Forest of Death right by the stream where Pearl found the coin. There are some things in life that are worth examining, then there are other times that you just thank the sweet Lord something ended up working out and you don't press your luck by questioning it.

"That was bloody dodgy!" Dr Cooke says, wiping his brow with the sleeve of his shirt.

"It felt like a million eyes were watching me in there," Clint finally manages to get out. "And that bloody horse wouldn't slow down! I screamed the whole way."

"City slickers," the Professor shakes his head.

"Right, well, we made it," I say, trying to shake off the foreboding thought that we have to go through it again to get back to Pearl's house.

Gingerly peeling off the knapsack from my back, I open it and retrieve the paper Pearl gave me this morning. I look down at the little hand drawn map on the lined paper and know we must be in the right place. There is a large rock formation by the stream in the shape of a whale, and the weeping willow tree she was sitting under when she uncovered the coin is in plain sight.

"She found it just under that tree," I say, pointing to the trunk where the roots are starting to come up out of the ground.

We take the reins of our horses and tie them each around a tree at the edge of the forest. I walk over to the riverbed and drop to my knees. The water is glistening, and I can make out some rocks at the bottom. Scooping my hand in, I lower my head and take a huge gulp of the icy cold liquid.

"It's very refreshing," I encourage the others, who start to follow suit.

After a few handfuls I sit back on my heels and look around. I can see why Pearl would pick a spot like this to just come and sit. It seems too close to paradise to be real. With the sounds of the water rushing over the gathering rocks at the top of the bank and the soft, plush grass surrounding it, the area seems untouched. The birds softly chirping as they fly overhead add to the idealness.

"Right, better get to it," I say once the others have finished with their drinks.

"You say it was over by this tree?" the Professor asks, walking over to stand beside me under the gigantic weeping willow. It appears John Wayne has left us for the time being.

"Right by that twisting root," I point to the ground. "Pearl said she was drawing in the dirt and her nail hit it."

"Could have been brought up from the water," Dr Cooke says, coming to stand beside us. "This tree is so close to the stream, the soil must be very moist. After time, the roots and soil get pushed up by the water, and it could have travelled with it. It's quite possible there are more under there…"

We all peer at the ground, thinking.

"After the train robbery, Butch and the Wild Bunch Gang rode off and dispersed. It would have made sense if he thought someone was hot on his tail to bury the coins somewhere and come back for them—they used to do that all the time. He had a cabin not too far from here in Brown's hole. It was surrounded by trails and caves so that law enforcement wouldn't be able to find them. They were famous for ditching their loot until things cooled down. Under this tree is the perfect spot. The only way to really get in here is through the forest, so it's not somewhere that would have been heavily visited, but it is remarkable enough to not forget where you buried the treasure," I explain.

"That's where a lot of these thieves went wrong," the Professor chimes in, putting his thumbs through his belt loops again and maintaining his fake American accent. "Damn fools kept forgetting where they buried their loot."

"Isn't Brown's Hole in Utah?" Clint says from behind us.

We all turn in amazement to look at him.

"How do you knot that?" I ask, impressed.

"I have Google," he says, holding up his phone.

"Put that down! You're supposed to be recording us," Dr Cooke says in outrage.

"I am," he says, pointing to his phone again. "It's got a camera on it."

"What about the bloody special lenses?" the Professor yells, momentarily losing his American accent.

"I've got built in filters on this," Clint holds up his phone as though we will be able to see something different about it. "Do you want me to give you a tan?"

"Not the bloody point!" the Professor yells at the same time Dr Cooke says "Go on then!".

"Brown's Hole is about a six hour car ride from here," Clint says, pressing more of the buttons on his phone. "Bit far to leave your gold, isn't it?"

I smile at him indulgently.

"Exactly what is wrong with technology," I say, looking to the Professor who is also nodding in agreement. "It gives you the *facts* without the *context*."

"My boy, that distance, what is it—about 500 miles?" the Professor, says and I nod. "Notice how I didn't even need your Google to calculate that… that is but a stroll in the park to the people of the late nineteenth century."

"Men would be gone for months at a time, to work on different projects like the railway or construction. It was only the people whose trades were of necessity to everyday life— farmers, blacksmiths, tailors—those were really the only people who lived and worked near their homes," I explain.

"Also, these modern roads weren't here, so instead of going around the land, they went through it on horseback," Dr Cooke adds.

"It says here on horseback it still takes eight hours to get to Brown's Hole," Clint turns the screen to show us. "Right here on Google maps."

"Would you stop using that bloody thing! That internal web nonsense is what is going to be the death of our profession. You watch one video and read a couple articles and everyone believes they can be the next bloody Indiana Jones—another thing we can thank the Yanks for," the Professor yells, trying to snatch the phone. "From now on, if you want to know anything, you will ask one of the three of us for the answer."

"What if you don't know the answer?" Clint asks.

The three of us look at each other, weighing up our answer.

"Well then it's not worth knowing," Dr Cooke finally says.

"And I want you to use that old camera we have supplied you, none of this new technology nonsense," the Professor says gruffly.

Clint doesn't say anything, but quietly puts his phone in his pocket and reaches into his bag for the old black camcorder. I wait for him to get it started before I continue.

"We know the coins must be somewhere in this region

of the country," I say, turning to the camera to explain my theory. "After the train robbery the Wild Bunch Gang had to disperse. The Pinkerton Detective agency was too close to tracking them down, so Butch Cassidy and the Sundance Kid along with his girlfriend Etta Place fled to Argentina. There was a shootout while they were living in Bolivia and that is where it is believed that Butch Cassidy died. They must have left the coins here because there isn't even a hint of one ever being sighted in South America."

"Don't most people believe the coins were buried in the Irish Canyons?" Clint asks from behind the camera, but cowers slightly at Dr Cooke's look of outrage.

"That was my question to ask to the camera and you know it!" Dr Cooke hisses.

"Well, it is the most likely choice," I say, trying to ignore the hostility between the two men and their intern. "But a lot of people don't believe that Butch Cassidy actually died in the shootout in Bolivia, they believe he managed to live under a false identity and died an old man in Utah. But that's all speculation—he could have just as likely lived out his days here, in Colorado. In which case, maybe he dug up the coins and reburied them here."

"But if he had all of these valuable coins why would he leave them buried? Why wouldn't he dig them up and spend them?" Clint asks in astonishment.

"Well, if he was trying to remain anonymous when he came back, he couldn't use the coins, could he? Someone

108

would have known who he was," I answer.

"What a waste," Clint says, looking at the ground where Pearl found the coin. "All those coins just sitting there, seems a bit pointless."

"See, that is the great thing about artefacts, my boy," the Professor says, rubbing his hands together. "A huge part of history is best guesses and speculation, but when you can place an artefact to a specific time or person it fills in those gaps and gives us more tangible leads."

"So better guesses?" Clint says, poking his head around the camera to look at the Professor.

"*Better guesses*," the Professor sputters in indignation and turns to Dr Cooke. "This younger generation has no respect for the art of archaeology. All sorts of faulty information from that bloody internet and they think they know everything. Who is actually in it for the knowledge anymore? They just want the riches, don't they, Daniel? We don't just get out a shovel and dig for gold, you know!" he finishes, turning to Clint, panting.

Clint looks a little affronted to be taking on the faults of his whole generation, but decides to not argue.

"I need a cup of tea," the Professor says. "And I'm taking off these chaps—never wear leather in the sun."

"Right, well we will have to come back with some tools tomorrow then," I say to the men.

"What kind of tools?" Clint asks from behind the camera.

"Well, tools to dig," I say, pointing to the ground.

"Kind of like shovels?" he says, and returns his face to behind the camera when he catches the Professor's eye.

Chapter Seven

My face is still a picture of exhilaration as I carefully get off the horse. Exhilaration or sheer terror from the recent trip through the forest of death... same thing.

With shaking hands I close the door of the stable and lift the saddle onto the shelf with the others. I'm not sure which one of us is more grateful to be rid of the other, but from the long snort the horse lets out I am guessing it's a closer tie than I originally thought.

"We made it," I say to the others.

"There's something living in that forest besides nature," Dr Cooke says, and I notice his eyes won't look back at where he has just come from.

"We have to do it all again tomorrow," Clint says in a near whimper.

"Oh, quit your whining!" the Professor dismounts from his horse and spits on the ground near his foot. The American accent is back in place but I notice his walk is laboured from the long ride and the ultra tight jeans.

"I think we could all do with a hot bath and a good night sleep," I say.

"Might get in some target practice first," the Professor says, tipping his hat to me and turning to make his way back to the bunkhouse.

I shoot a frightened look to Dr Cooke.

"I'll do what I can," he says to me before following the Professor.

"And I'll watch the two of them," Clint says to me reassuringly, turning to follow Dr Cooke before I hear him mutter under his breath. "Honestly, I don't know which one is worse…"

Turning around I head back to the main house, thinking about the little we accomplished today and the exhilaration I feel. I can't seem to stem the anticipation of tomorrow and what we might possibly uncover. Once I am close to the back of the property I take a last look at the sinking sun and stop when I see what looks like a solitary figure in the far distance at the front of the property, close to the main road. When I squint the black shape takes a slightly clearer form and I can see that there are actually two people who are just standing close together. I stop and squint my eyes more, seeing if I can make out whether it is Griffin and Pearl when I jump at a snapping noise beside me from a small bush. Taking a step back, I look around to see if anyone is in the vicinity that could have caused the noise, but when I see that no one is around me I tell myself to relax. I'm just worked up from the creepy forest. It's probably nothing.

But then the bush shakes, and I take another step back.

Whatever is in there isn't a small woodland creature. Just when I decide to dash into the house through the back door I hear a sharp curse.

Someone is in the bush. Looking around again I take a tentative step towards it.

"Hello?" I ask, but the bush stays silent.

I take another step towards it, and another, but nothing moves in it. The small circular bush isn't very big, just dense—and now that I am up close to it, I can see its full circumference and there isn't anyone around it. I put one hand on the top of the branches, deciding my mind is playing tricks on me after being in the forest of death, and pull back one of the branches to assure myself that I had imagined everything. Before my hand is able to complete the action, the branches part and a huge figure pops out of the top of the bush like a jack in the box.

"Ah!" I yell, clutching my chest. "What the hell are you *doing?*"

Griffin's torso looks like it is floating on top of the thick, dense hedge as he puts his finger to his lip to indicate for me to be quiet.

"What the hell do you *think* I am doing?" he hisses, as though in this situation I am the crazy one. "*Investigating.*"

"What?" I look him up and down and realize that this inspection clarifies nothing. His face is covered in a black, greasy substance with leaves stuck in his hair and his green long sleeves shirt covered in dirt. "What's that on your face?

"Your mascara," he shoos away the question like it's a pesky fly with one hand as his other grips a pair of binoculars. "Quickly, move away before she sees you!"

"Before who sees me?" I ask, looking around.

"*Pearl*, who do you think?" Griffin asks in a tone of frustration

"You're spying on Pearl?" I ask him. "Why?"

"You told me to keep an eye out for something suspicious, so that's what I'm doing. There's something not normal about that woman."

"And this," I say, indicating his appearance, "is completely normal?"

"Joke all you want, but I'm doing this for you," he says, and then leans backwards to get a better view of the people by the main road. "She's been meeting people all day," he mumbles to me.

"Well, I expect they're here to buy the drugs," I say to him.

"June, I drove a taxi for the better part of my adult life, I think I know a drug deal when I see one," he says, shaking his head at me like I don't know what I'm talking about. "Only some of them were buying drugs. Some are here for something else…"

"What are you talking about?" I ask as panic rises in my chest. "Who? How do you know? What did they say?"

The questions reel off as my mind comes up with the possibilities. What if the Historical Society sent someone to check up on me? Has Oxford found out what I've done.?

"Some people came and gave her money and they got a bag full of green stuff—is that clear enough for you?" he asks. "Then others—like this bloke—came just for a chat."

"Maybe they're her neighbours," I say to him.

"No, they would have come to the front door like the customers," he says, shaking his head while still looking in Pearl's direction. "She's met three people today at the end of her driveway. She's obviously arranged a meeting with them because they stand there and wait for her to come."

"That does sound odd," I say, trying to see if I can make out who Pearl is talking to.

"Well, I wouldn't call it normal," he says, turning to look at me.

"Did you hear anything they said?" I grab his sleeve.

"Not much. But I could have sworn a man said he would "Send her packing,"

"Oh God," I say, grabbing my stomach.

"They can't do this to you, June." Griffin says grabbing my arm. "I know I gave you a hard time on the plane, but if that Phillip comes and tries to pack you off anywhere I'll be the first one there to tell him who will be leaving! You've got the support of Oxford behind you, they gave you this job and there's nothing he can do about it."

I fight the sob that tries to escape from my throat and turn to Griffin. I need to tell him, before they come and escort me off the property.

"I'm so proud of you June," he says, putting his hands on my arms and ducking his head so our eyes are even. "I know you were frustrated with everything that was happening back home, but look what you've accomplished! When everyone was telling you to forget it, you took it on the chin, and you *earned* this doing it your way. And the way you handled the whole drug thing—I thought for sure you were going to pack it in. But you didn't and I'm not going to let some jealous jerk take that away from you!"

My chin wobbles as I stare at him.

"It will all be alright," he says gathering me into his arms, and I squeeze him so tightly to me.

It's finally happening, Griffin holding me like this, spending his day trying to protect me. We are finally getting closer to each other without all of the inhibitions of home. And I am about to throw a grenade into it.

"Griffin, there's something I need to tell—"

"*June and her man friend, sitting in a tree,*" I hear the sing-song voice from behind me and jump, nearly knocking Griffin and myself over.

I turn to look at Pearl who is rocking back and forth on the balls of her feet with a large grin on her face.

"I—I didn't hear you come up," I say to her.

"Just been talking to a friend," she says, pointing to where she just came from.

"A friend?" Griffin asks, his protective arm tightening around my waist.

She looks from Griffin to me, frowning.

"Yeah, Bill, he lives just a few ranches down. A bunch of us are putting in a bulk order for supplies. He's ordered me some picket pins."

"Some, what?" I ask.

"Picket pins. You hook your horse up to them and they can wander in the pasture without having to worry about them going off. Much cheaper than fencing and won't affect my view. Bill's got them being sent to me."

Something clicks in my mind and my body relaxes. "He's going to *send her picket pins*," I say to Griffin.

"Picket pins, right," he says nodding, though I can see he isn't as relieved by the news as me. "I suppose that sounds right."

"I'm gonna get dinner started. Steak and potatoes tonight," Pearl says, walking away from us before finishing her sentence.

"That's what you must have overheard," I say to Griffin, laughing.

"Maybe," he says, his narrow eyes following Pearl into the house. "But, there's just something not right here. I can feel it in my bones."

Looking at him with the smeared mascara on his face, the corner of my mouth lifts. He did this for me. He spent his whole day outside in this cold, damp bush for me. Because he believes in me and wants to protect me.

And I'm going to make him proud of me, for the right

reasons.

"I think I am going to find the coins," I say to him.

"You do? What did you find today?" he asks, his attention momentarily diverted from Pearl.

"Nothing yet," I say, shaking my head. "I guess I just have a feeling."

His face splits into a grin. "Of course you will, and don't worry about anything here. I'm on it. I'll find out what's going on."

I pull him close to me again to hide my face.

Chapter Eight

"I've got all the tools packed," I say, entering the kitchen and seeing everyone gathered around the table. "The horse wasn't too happy about the buggy strapped to his back but I couldn't think of another way to get all the shovels and brushes and equipment there. I don't think a car can make it through that forest."

I repress the shudder just thinking about the forest. There is just something about the weeping branches nearly touching the floor as they sway in the breeze. They remind me of long fingers toying with me as they threaten to reach out and snatch. I just want to get through it as quickly as possible and I don't relish the thought of how much the buggy will probably slow down the process. The only silver lining is there is a small seat on the front, just big enough for one person, so at least I won't have to sit on the horse's back again. I much prefer the idea of four wheels under me to four temperamental legs.

"And now there's twenty-eight!" the Professor gleefully points to the computer screen he, Dr Cooke, and Griffin are huddled around.

"See that little button in the corner that looks like a broken circle with an arrow?"

"The refresh button?" Griffin asks, sitting behind the computer.

"Is that what it's called?" Dr Cooke asks and then shrugs. "A very logical name for it, actually."

"Click it!" the Professor urges him, and then lets out another gleeful sound when Griffin does it. "Twenty-nine now!"

"We're famous!" Dr Cooke yells as he and the Professor exchange pleased looks with each other. "We are finally being appreciated."

"What's this all about?" I say, pushing my way into the huddle.

"Clifford's unloaded our video from yesterday onto the internet," the Professor says and taps Griffin on the shoulder. "Again my boy."

"Thirty!" Dr Cooke says, unnecessarily pointing to the screen. "Thirty people have viewed the video now!"

The floor seems to move underneath me and I grab for the back of the chair.

"What video?" I say in alarm.

"The video of us by the site," Dr Cooke explains, pressing a key on the computer.

"The one—" I try and stay calm as the bile rises up in my throat. "The one of us talking about the excavation?"

"Clifford's done a little montage of it all so far," the

Professor says, beaming at Clint as he walks through the door. "He got some very good angles of me."

"You—you put it on the *internet?*" My head vibrates as I seethe with anger.

"Er—yeah…" Clint replies in a cautious tone.

"Of all the—" the slur of curse words that comes out of my mouth makes Dr Cooke's cheeks turn scarlet.

"June!" Griffin gasps.

"She didn't learn those from me," the Professor shakes his head at Dr Cooke.

"You take it down!" I say, lunging to grab Clint by the front of his shirt. I shake him, my face inches from his own. "You take it down right now!"

"June!" Griffin puts his arm around my waist and lifts me away from Clint so my legs are flailing in the air.

"Do you hear me? You take it down right now or I'll come over there and kick that skinny jean clad ass!" I scream, still flailing in Griffin's arms.

"June, what's got into you?" the Professor frowns.

"They made me do it!" Clint cowers away from me and points his bony finger at the Professor.

I stop flailing and put my feet on the ground, shifting my body to look in the Professor's direction.

"I told you not to send in the bloody thing until we are home. You gave me your word!" I yell at him, my voice choked with tears from the shock.

"Well, I didn't know you would take us all to the

gallows," the Professor shrugs. "Clifford mentioned this MyTube to us yesterday, and it sounded intriguing. If you get ten thousand views they pay you!"

"Who has seen it?" I ask. Griffin relaxes his grip but his arm stays wrapped around me.

"Well, let's see," the Professor says and clicks a button. "Thirty-one now! I must admit I didn't have much faith in this internet video idea, but obviously there are many people in the world who were desperate for some actual fact-based knowledge."

"I've always said we have a lot to offer the modern world, haven't I, Albert? I knew this new generation wasn't lost forever. I mean, alright, most of this Millennial generation are real gits, but obviously there are some rubies in the woodwork. They must have been sitting at home, just waiting for something of this substance to come along onto their computer."

The Professor leans over Dr Cooke and presses a button. "Thirty-two!"

"I really should send for some more hats," Dr Cooke says idly, chewing on his bottom lip. "I had no clue we would have this sort of fan base. I can't *believe* I left my bowler at home."

"I'd love to send this to that bloody university," the Professor stares at the screen. "I'd like to see them turn us down for funding now."

"No one is sending it to the university!" I yell. "I mean

it, you take that down right now before anyone else sees it!"

"We don't need them, Albert! Today it's..." Dr Cooke says, leaning over the computer and clicking the mouse. "Thirty-three! Tomorrow it's the world!"

I turn to look at Clint, who looks terribly frightened of me.

"I'll take it down now," he assures me, bobbing his head.

"But our fans!" the Professor argues.

I turn on him and give him a look of contempt. "If I hear one more word about you posting any of these bloody videos before we get home, I will personally make sure there isn't a drop of whiskey left in Britain when we return—"

"Well, there's no need for that," the Professor looks affronted and sits up straight. "Very uncalled for."

"Oh God, if anyone saw that," I say, my hand shaking as I bring it to my mouth.

"June, what is going on?" Griffin asks me in a low voice. "I've never seen you like this."

"I'm... I'm under a contract," I say the first thing that pops into my head. "If Oxford saw that... if the Historical Society saw that..."

"No one saw it but them," Griffin says, stroking my arm while studying my face.

My cheeks still feel as if they're on fire. "It just has to come down."

"It will," he nods to me and then looks at Clint.

"Fine, I'll do it now," Clint says, and makes his way

around the table to the computer.

The Professor crosses his arms over his chest and makes a sulking face.

"It's alright," Griffin says to me, lifting my chin. "You alright?"

I can see the worry on his face and realize how out of character my little outburst must seem to them. I force the corners of my mouth up and sigh.

"Okay, you're right. I—I overreacted," I say, forcing a small laugh.

Dr Cooke sniffs.

"But no more uploading anything onto the internet," I warn them, pointing my finger.

"Whatever you say," the Professor shrugs, not turning his face to mine.

"We better get going. I've got the horses ready," I remind them.

The Professor gets up and walks past me without saying anything.

"Right, come on Clifford—er, Clint, sorry," Dr Cooke says, standing up from the computer. "Griffin, my lad, will you be joining us today?"

"No, I think I will hold down the fort here, today," he says to Dr Cooke, and shoots me a wink.

"You're sure you don't want to come?" I ask.

"No, I have a few things I have to take care of," he says, and quickly adds, "you know—for the screenplay."

The fact that he chose to explain makes me think he has other things that he will be working on apart from the screenplay. Pleased that he is trying to look out for me, but worried about how far his "digging" will go, I nod and place a kiss on his cheek.

"Carlton, you have the video camera?" the Professor asks, his head poking through the back door. "That is, if we are still allowed to record?"

His eyes dart to me briefly, and I narrow my own at his snide tone.

"As long as it stays off the internet you can do whatever the bloody hell you want with your camera," I say in a falsely sweet tone.

"Fully charged," Clint nods to him.

"I'm just going to run and get my Stetson!" Dr Cooke rushes out of the kitchen, and from the little window I see his small squat form hurdling over the back lawn to the bunkhouse.

"And you have some form of a backup battery as well, I assume?" the Professor says to Clint as they both start to make their way out of the kitchen. "Is there perhaps some sort of portable outlet you have in case you need to plug it in?"

Their voices drift further away as they make their way over the back lawn in the direction of the stables.

"Well, I better go too," I say, pointing to the open doorway. I suddenly feel very tired considering I woke up not too long ago

"You'll do great today," Griffin says, lifting my chin with his finger.

"Thanks," I smile back.

"I love you," he says, and I can see he is waiting for me to respond before kissing me.

"I love you, too," I whisper.

Chapter Nine

We break through the last of the forest and emerge into the clearing. I lift up my glasses and rub my eyes, trying to adjust them to the sunlight.

I thought the journey through the forest would be better if I wasn't sitting on that bloody horse, but the wagon provided no protection from the eerie atmosphere. In some ways it was worse, as it took much longer to pass through and all that kept running through my head was what would happen if the horse got free and decided to bolt.

The chatter from the Professor and Dr Cooke proved to be a welcome distraction. Not that I could hear exactly what they were saying; they kept whispering to each other and looking back over their shoulders in my direction, but the noise was a welcome distraction.

There's got to be a better way of getting to this place.

"I'm not entirely sure, but I don't think that is the way we came yesterday," I say to the others as I pull the horse to a stop, and start to climb down before reaching back for my knapsack. "I remember hurtling over a massive tree yesterday and we never came upon it today."

"I wish I had jumped over something," Clint says,

looking much better than he did this time yesterday. He even managed to gel his hair this morning and he's wearing ridiculously tight jeans that make his legs look like long twigs sticking out of his torso. "My horse took me through some sort of swamp. It was disgusting."

"I think we passed that large tree earlier June, close to where that old circular rock gathering was," Dr Cooke says as he starts fiddling with the white scarf tied around his neck. "I still say that could be remnants from the Wild Bunch Gang—I can just imagine them sitting around a camp fire, discussing their latest heists."

"It was a well, I tell you," the Professor states, buttoning up his tan coloured vest. "It explains why the rocks were stacked so closely and on top of each other."

"It was probably just a pile of rocks," Clint mumbles, obviously bored with the debate we've all been listening to for the past twenty minutes. "Who lights a fire or builds a well in the middle of a forest?"

Clint sticks a piece of gum between his teeth before grabbing the camera out of the bag.

"Oh!"

I see both the Professor and Dr Cooke perk up at the sight, no longer fiddling with their attire and immediately taking on an air of authority. They both plaster on a smile and freeze in their current positions, waiting for the camera to turn on. Clint seems to take the hint and points it in their direction.

Let them be excited about it, I think. As long as they don't post anything on the internet, what harm is there in them filming?

I take a sideways look at the camera, not trusting it.

"Well, my dear lad, as you can see behind us, this forest is of great diversity in age. Some trees are hundreds of years old, whereas others seem to only be from this last century," the Professor dramatically sweeps his hand over the scenery behind him like a model on the home shopping channel.

"Some of these trees might not have even been here during Butch Cassidy's day." Dr Cooke quickly ambles up beside the Professor. "The fire hole in question—"

"Or more likely, the *well*," the Professor interjects, taking a small step forward and positioning himself in front of Dr Cooke.

Dr Cooke quickly rights this.

"It might have been in the open a century ago. It's not too far from here, and you can see these trees are much smaller than those in the centre of the forest. This is due to the trees self-seeding—which, for those who don't know," Dr Cooke turns with a dazzling smile to the camera, lifting his chin at a very uncomfortable angle. "Is when the seeds of one tree scatter and then get covered in the ground, enabling roots to form."

"Also, broken branches can often act as shoots, with the same result," the Professor adds, shuffling closer to Dr Cooke.

"Or the roots themselves can branch out," Dr Cooke says, stepping so close to the Professor that they seem to be joined at the hip.

"The possibilities are endless," the Professor says, and turns to Dr Cooke smiling.

Neither of them seem to know what to say next, and an uncomfortable silence fills the air. I can see from the puzzled looks on their faces they are both racking their brains for more tree facts.

"Right, well, I'm sure your fans will be enthralled," I say, standing behind Clint with my arms folded over my chest. "But perhaps we should get started?"

Turning from them, I stride over to the willow tree.

I study the roots that are peeking out from the ground. I bite my bottom lip in concentration as I think about the best way to go about this.

"So what's the plan?" Clint asks from behind me.

This is it. It's finally my chance to prove what I am capable of. *Just don't look like a prat on the camera,* I warn myself.

I push my glasses up the bridge of my nose and straighten my trench coat before turning to stare into the camera lens.

"In archaeology, we usually begin with a trial excavation. We don't know what is beneath the soil and we don't want to disturb any potential findings," I say, my hand sweeping in an arc to indicate the tree behind me. It's not lost on me that I just mocked the Professor for doing the same thing.

"This helps us gauge what we may find when digging in a large area, and also what care we need to take to preserve the integrity of the site."

"Aren't you just looking for the coins, though?" Clint asks, peering over the top of the camera. "You think there could be other stuff down there?"

"Well, in this case, probably not. Usually these trenches are done to protect the *unknown*. See, archaeology not only helps uncover lost treasure, but it also helps fill in the gaps of history with *how* things were buried." Walking over to the tree I crouch down by the trunk to look at the earth, my bum resting on the heel of my brown boots. "Before the fourth millennium writing hadn't been invented and so much of the time before is lost. Sometimes we can learn quite a bit about a society by their rituals and from this how they buried things—the positioning, the wrapping—all helps add context to the people and their culture."

"Quite right, June," the Professor says, coming to crouch down beside me, but staring at the camera the whole time. Dr Cooke quickly appears on my other side.

"Seeing how some cultures buried their artefacts helps determine their customs, which hopefully can be linked to other groups' customs, and that provides historians with links," Dr Cooke says, bringing his fingers together as though talking to a small child.

"And those links help fill in the gaps in history, until one day we are able to connect all of the dots and have a firm grasp on all that has been accomplished in this great world," the Professor finishes, both men looking into the camera, waiting for their profound words to sink in.

"The good news for us," I say, interrupting the reverence while managing not to roll my eyes at the pair of them, "Is the fact that we already have plenty of *context* about Butch Cassidy. That period in history was well recorded. His life, however has garnered sensationalist history, and what we are presented as facts could just be false propaganda from the time, so there is always history to be gained. Also, if the treasure is not buried here, we don't want to disturb anything that might give us a clue as to where it could be buried."

"Like a treasure map?" Clint says with much enthusiasm.

I smile at his reaction. He's about the same age as my first year students. They also seem more attentive in lectures when the word 'treasure' is mentioned.

"Like soil conditions," I say, standing up straight and dusting off my hands on the front of my pants. "If we can see the soil has settled, or there are small tunnels where water has flowed through, it could help us determine whether we need to dig lower, or somewhere else entirely."

"Oh," Clint says nodding. "So, now what?"

"Now we dig," I say, looking to the other men as I peel off my trench coat and push up the sleeves of my plaid shirt. "A shovel a piece then, gents?"

"Oh June dear," Dr Cooke looks suddenly hesitant, first making sure the stark white scarf is in place before putting his hand on his back. "I—er—my back you know…"

I turn to the Professor with my eyebrow raised.

The Professor tugs on the bottom of his neatly pressed vest and adjusts his hat.

"You know June Bug, I have been meaning to catch up on my journal," the Professor pulls it out from the inside pocket of his coat. "The doctor did say it was important."

I cross my arms, staring at him.

"Why don't you ask Oxford to send you some manual labour?" the Professor says, looking around. "Usually you'd have lackeys for this sort of thing."

"They—er—offered," I say, nodding. "But I wanted to take a more hands on approach… this being my first dig and all."

The Professor looks unconvinced.

"And I was told you two would be all the help I need if you remember correctly," I point out.

"Well, naturally I would, if only I didn't have so much writing to catch up on," the Professor says, holding the journal up.

"I could help with that, Albert," Dr Cooke says, grasping onto the suggestion and coming to stand beside the Professor. "Where have you left off?"

"As we landed, Daniel," the Professor says, opening the journal. "I was hoping by putting it off a bit I would have forgotten that bloody car ride, but no such luck, I'm afraid."

"Oh, yes. Well, sound logic if nothing else," Dr Cooke

says and the two of them start to make their way back to the horses.

"Brilliant," I say, throwing my arms up in the air at them. *You need us June Bug,* they said, *you can't do this without us.*

"Aren't you supposed to have people to dig for you?" Clint asks, and I notice the camera is still pointing directly at my face.

Caught off guard by the question, I smooth my hands over the front of my shirt to gain time.

"Well, not necessarily... I mean, this is only the exploratory stage," I say, looking down at the floor of the tree.

To be honest, I should have a whole team with me. If this were being funded by the University I would have. Phillip *bloody* Hurst would have all the people and machinery in the world at his beck and call. I rub my foot over the tight compacted dirt under me and realize my plan might have developed a few more snags. I mean, if I can't manage it with my own two hands I'm in a bit of sticky water. It's not like I can rent excavators and hire labour. I don't have any money and wouldn't even know how to get that sort of machinery here.

"So, where are you going to dig?" Clint asks.

I look up at his expectant face and decide to just get started with it and worry about the what-ifs when they happen.

"Well, first, I'll do a small sweep of the area with a metal detector," I say, walking over to the wagon to retrieve the flimsy metal detector I found in Pearl's shed. She said she sometimes liked to walk the canyons with it, and once I established it actually worked, I thought it a waste to go out and get another one from the shops.

"The top layer of soil is usually artificial, meaning it won't hold any real significant artefacts. The earth settles over time and with the running water beside it, I'm sure the top portion of this soil would get a new layer quite often considering the roots aren't protruding too much out of the ground. But Pearl found the coin's edge peeking out of the ground so you never know…"

I walk back to the area under the tree and lift the metal detector and start to wave it over the ground. Frowning at the lack of noise, I look down and realize my mistake.

Turning the bloody thing on might help.

I clear my throat and try and flick the switch without anyone seeing. I wave it over the ground again, and hear a constant short beeping sound, but no metal is detected. I turn around and catch the two men peering over, but when they see I'm looking they quickly put their heads together again and look at the journal.

I have a good mind to post those videos back on the Internet so everyone can see what a wonderful help they are.

"And now we dig!" I say enthusiastically to Clint.

"We?" he asks, raising his eyebrows and pointing to the camera. "I've got to hold this."

"Oh bloody well then, *I'll* dig."

Like he could do anything in those ridiculous pants anyways. And who wears a ribbed turtleneck on an excavation site?

After only a few shovels of dirt I can feel the hot sun on the back of my neck and I wipe my forehead.

"We dig trenches to start instead of holes in order to get a better sense of the area—not limiting ourselves to one spot," I explain, heaving the dirt. "Might not help us in this case, as Butch Cassidy would have most likely buried the coins together in some sort of bag, but you never know—better to be safe than sorry. You've got to start somewhere!" I try to sound enthusiastic, but I'm already huffing and puffing from the exertion.

I pierce the ground again with the spade's blade and put my foot on the back to push it further into the earth. Time seems to creep by slowly, at least, it feels that way as the hot sun rises higher and higher. The two men are engrossed in their task under a nearby tree, but every so often I catch one of them peeking over at my progress until they catch me watching and quickly look away.

I'm not exactly sure how I expected my first excavation project to go, but I would like to think I had a bit higher expectations than this.

"You know, Butch Cassidy's start to crime wasn't as glamorous as most people think," I say over my shoulder to Clint, panting now as I shovel, the trench now as deep as my knees and about five feet long. "He went into a store in the town next to the one he was living in. He needed a new pair of pants but it was closed, so he took the pants and a slice of pie and left an IOU note. The store owner pressed charges."

I push back the now damp curling tendrils from around my face and readjust my glasses. "He was acquitted at trial, but then moved to Colorado because of it. That's where he met Matt Wainer at the horse tracks, and Matt became his first partner in crime."

Clutching a stitch in my side, I lean on the shovel.

"See that's the thing I love most about history. You not only get to figure out what happened and put it all in order, but you also get to think about what *could* have happened. What would have happened if the store owner hadn't pressed charges? Would Butch have gone to Colorado?" I pick up the shovel again and dig it into the ground. "People make choices for all sorts of reasons, and we get to figure out what those reasons were."

"You actually really like this stuff, huh?" Clint asks, now leaning on a tree as though tired of standing, both hands now supporting the small camera.

"I love *this stuff*. It's challenging, of course. And you do have to get your hands dirty sometimes!" I yell in the direction of the two men. "But, the hunt is all a part of the fun. Hey—I've hit something!"

I throw the shovel aside and get down on my hands and knees. The Professor and Dr Cooke come running over and

I take out a brush from my knapsack and carefully start dusting the earth. After a few more strokes I sit down in my freshly dug trench.

"Rock," I sigh in exasperation.

"Hmm, yes, it seems so," the Professor says from above me.

I shoot him a withering stare. I think I am capable of determining what a rock is.

"Shall we have lunch?" Dr Cooke asks, wiping his brow with a white handkerchief. "It seems like a long time since breakfast."

"And you two must be famished!" I spit out.

"Well, yes, if you must know," says the Professor. "Chester, my lad, you must be ready for a break?"

"Absolutely," Clint says, lowering the camera and stretching his neck to the side.

"Excellent, go and retrieve the basket from the wagon," the Professor demands and turns back to inspect the trench I've dug.

After I eat the sandwiches and piece of cake Pearl packed for our lunch, I feel a renewed sense of energy.

"I've dug the big one now," I say to the others, picking up the shovel. "The two little ones left shouldn't take long."

This proves to be an optimistic statement. The roots around the tree end up being very troublesome as I hack away at the earth, sweating profusely in the afternoon heat. The two older men find a tree to sit under not too far from where I'm digging and manage to dose off—*lazy buggers*.

Clint keeps up a stream of conversation, and I'm not sure if it is meant to encourage me or to keep himself from boredom.

"So you think Butch Cassidy moved the treasure then, after the robbery?" Clint asks, wiping his own brow; sweat has caused his carefully gelled hair to droop in a greasy mess over his forehead. "I thought you said it was buried in the Irish Canyon?"

"Well, that's not too far from here. And it's well known they used to hide their loot until they could come back at a safer time to claim it. They had a secret hide out called Robbers Roost that they used to go to after a robbery or during the winter. There were such narrow passageways into it that no one could sneak up on you without being seen," I explain, now starting work on the second trench. "If Butch didn't die in Bolivia, I think the first thing he would have done when he got back to Colorado was dig up the coins and move them, and this seems like a spot that would really appeal to him."

I look around at the small clearing, taking note of the single entry point through the forest. The tall rock formations that cocoon the area would make it next to impossible to gain a different entrance to this secret paradise.

I stretch my neck back and look up at the tall grey walls; even in today's age you would be hard pressed to come that way unless you were an excellent climber or had a helicopter.

But that would've never been a concern for Butch Cassidy in the early twentieth century.

"There's a history museum not too far from their old hideout. It might be worth us going to have a look," I say as I shove the spade into the ground and throw the dirt off to the side again.

Something in the movement catches my eye and I look around to see a reflection in the brown dirt.

I throw the shovel down, push my glasses up and crouch down beside the dirt.

"I've—I've found something," I say under my breath, and then turn to yell to the others. "I've found something!"

For two men with back troubles and all other ailments known to man, they're awake and are at my side within seconds.

"Is it another coin?" Dr Cooke asks, his hat still crooked from the nap. The Professor looks wrinkly and dishevelled, making me realize how bad I must look, considering I'm the one who's done all the hard labour.

"No," I say, lifting up the small piece between my dirt-stained fingers to show them. "It's a key."

"A key to what?" Clint asks, and I pull my face back as the camera lens is positioned inches from it.

"I—I don't know," I shake my head. "I've only just found it!"

"Well let's have a closer look," the Professor says, peering at my fingers and straining his eyes.

I take out a white handkerchief from my back pocket and gingerly place the key on top of it.

"Three circles, all connected," Dr Cooke breathes, rubbing his chin. "That's the Borromean Ring, isn't it Albert?"

"The what?" Clint tries to get his face closer to see the key.

"It's a Christian symbol, it represents the Holy Trinity," the Professor explains, never taking his eyes off the key. "It represents the Father, Son and Holy Spirit."

"But this looks a little oval to me," I say, pulling my face back a bit to get another angle on the key. "The blade itself is just a standard two prong, it could fit anything."

The key is no longer than my pinkie finger, making it unlikely to be for a door; more likely a small lock or latch of some kind.

"It's not a perfect circle, no," Dr Cooke concedes as the three of us huddle around it, Clint trying to get the closest. "And they don't seem to be all uniform in size."

"It could just be the tools and skill that was available to make it," the Professor argues, wiping the back of his neck with his own handkerchief. "We won't know until we can clean it up and have a better look at the markings on it."

I look up at the sky and see that the bright sun has started to fade behind the clouds.

"I think we should cover the trenches and come back tomorrow," I say to the men and I carefully stand up. I hold onto the key as though it is something fragile and delicate. "This key opens something, and it could very well be buried deeper down there."

I point to the area where I've spent the day digging.

"Right," the Professor nods and turns to Clint. "Go and get the tarp and weights so we can cover this."

Clint rushes off to the wagon and I look back down at the key, still feeling a bit amazed by it.

Alright, I know it's not the treasure, but half way through that second trench with little to no resources I was starting to think I might be on a bit of a wild goose chase here. But standing here, holding this key, I feel a sense of excitement. Relief seeps through my veins, and the anxiety about what I have done to get here seems far away.

My first discovery.

"By George, this is exciting," Dr Cooke claps his hands together. "I'd almost forgotten what this feels like, eh Albert?"

The Professor smiles down at the key before wrapping his arm around Dr Cooke's shoulders.

"There are some things, Daniel, that are impossible to forget."

Chapter Ten

We spend the next week excavating a three metre radius all around the tree, with no luck. After the first day, my hands were covered in blisters and I could hardly move. Griffin took pity on me and joined us the next day, more than willing to put off his writing to help me dig. A decision I think he greatly regretted once we had dug the hole so deep we had to find some rope so he could climb back out again.

In the end we had to admit defeat, or at least acknowledge that neither the coins or what the key belonged to were around the tree.

"But what if it's only another foot below!" Griffin argued, looking at the area that created a large moat around the weeping willow.

"He wouldn't have buried the key a foot below the surface and the coins over six feet deep," I argued.

"But what's the key for, then?"

A thought that had been plaguing me for the past week. What was the key for, and was it just a coincidence it was found where the coin was? What if it's just something that was dropped and means absolutely nothing? My intuition keeps rejecting this thought. It's too much of a coincidence. The coin and the key have to be related, and I *am* going to figure out how.

We trudge back to Pearl's house and I get ready for bed. Sitting in bed, I study a book on Christian iconography. After cleaning the key we all agreed that the circles weren't equal in size and they did appear to be more of ovals than true circles. The key was roughly made, the welding marks were amateur at best, meaning it could very well be circles that were poorly crafted. And not a single marking—no letters or numbers to indicate what it could possibly be for.

"But he was Mormon," I say aloud, more to myself than to Griffin, who is lying beside me, writing furiously on his notepad. He's had a bit of a brainwave since yesterday morning and has written half a notepad worth of material for the screenplay. He also hasn't slept in two days which I don't think is very advisable, but I'm choosing not to comment.

"Hmm?" Griffin looks up absently from his papers to look at me. "Did you say something?"

"Why would he have a Christian symbol on this key? He wasn't religious, he came from a Mormon background, but he was never known to show much inclination toward his faith."

"Maybe he had a 'come to Jesus' moment in Bolivia when he was getting shot at," Griffin shrugs and returns to his work.

"Perhaps," I say, but without any real enthusiasm.

Griffin is hunched over beside me and I don't think his pen is able to keep up with his mind as it whirls across the page. His floppy brown hair has lightened just a touch from his days in the hot sun, his shoulders tanned from all the digging without his shirt on.

I, on the other hand, have a very burnt neck and face, but the rest of me that was diligently covered with clothing looks almost translucent in comparison.

"I must be missing something," I say, shaking my head and racking my brain, picturing all the information I attained on Butch Cassidy before we left England. Not one photo, not one description in any of the historical accountings, mentioned a symbol like this. Closing my eyes, the book pages appear on my eyelids, my eyes scanning them as I swipe each away onto the next piece of information. *Nothing.* Yet the coin is from the robbery. I'm sure of it. But how is the key connected?

"There's a museum not too far from here dedicated to the old west. I've heard it has some remarkable pieces in it from Butch Cassidy's life, and a good collection of artefacts from the Wild Bunch Gang. Maybe it has something..." I put the book on my bedside table and tuck my hair behind my ears.

"Done!" Griffin says triumphantly as he pulls the pen from the page in a flourish.

"You finished?" I say incredulously. "The whole screenplay?"

"No, the detailed outline," Griffin says, neatly stacking the pages together. "But now it's just a matter of writing it all out."

"And you wouldn't find it helpful to borrow Clint's computer?" I offer again.

"Don't trust them," he says, shaking his head. "Not after last time."

"Last time being in your Year 11?" I ask him.

"June, I didn't get to do my science A levels because of my computer crashing. Lost my whole project the night before it was due. Think of where I might be today if I'd been able to hand that in."

"You told me you were failing anyways," I point out. "And computers have come a long way since then. At home mine gets backed up every night to the Cloud."

"Don't trust it," Griffin shakes his head. "Pen and paper or the trusty typewriter for me."

I look at the bulky machine in the corner of the room that we had to pay fifty pounds in freight costs to get over here. He hasn't taken the cover off of it once.

"The Professor seems to be doing better since we got here," I say to him, playing with a loose thread on the coverlet.

"They've taken a fancy to that camera," he says.

"Hmm, well as long as it stays off the Internet I don't care what they do with it," I smile. Every time I get excited or raise my voice I see Clint cower away from me a bit. As he should. *Don't test me* is the message I want ingrained in his head.

Yesterday the two men did a rather long-winded piece where they acted out how they imagined Butch Cassidy and the Sundance Kid raced from the robbery and buried their loot. The Professor won the coin flip to play Butch, and Dr Cooke begrudgingly played the Sundance Kid. It was all very innocent until the Professor got a hold of a real gun from Pearl's gun collection and nearly shot the mule, Dolly, pretending she was a lawman after them.

Now that would be a YouTube sensation.

"So will you take us?" I ask Griffin, pulling up the cover and nestling into the crook of his arm.

"Take you where?" he asks.

"To the Butch Cassidy museum," I say to him. "It's not far from here, about an hour I think. We could go tomorrow if you're free."

"I could do that," he says nodding. "Though I'm not sure the others would be up for the drive."

"Oh, they'll be up for it," I say, putting my hand on his chest. "They'll love getting to tour the museum on camera, showing how knowledgeable they are."

Griffin nods, running his fingertips up and down the side of my arm.

"Can I ask you something?" I tilt my head back to look up at him.

"Hmm," he murmurs, kissing my lips.

"Do you think I nag you too much?"

He suddenly stops the action and pulls his face back.

"Er... why do you ask?" I can tell from the tone of his voice he isn't sure how to answer.

"It's just, when Clint was showing me some of the footage on his computer yesterday... I don't know, I just noticed how I tend to be the voice of gloom in them," I shrug, looking down.

To be honest, I've been watching the videos back every night since that day Clint uploaded it onto the Internet. It finally dawned on me that the people who gave the funding to the Professor and Dr Cooke would be watching the videos—watching me. Now, I'm not sure how they will react if they discover what I've done—honestly I have enough things to worry about without adding the British Archaeological Association into the mix. I just thought that if everything goes to pot and I'm fired someone would watch the videos and see that I am not completely useless. That given the chance I have a lot of talent and knowledge to give to the world. But watching the videos is a lot like hearing your own voice back on a recording. My first instinct was 'that's not how I act, surely'. I act so... well, *prudish*. But honestly, the Professor could have killed someone yesterday. And when I yelled at Griffin the other day for bumping into me, causing me to fall into the freshly dug hole, I was only doing the *responsible* thing. I could have broken my neck, or worse, disturbed some buried artefact. And I am under a lot of stress right now.

"June, you aren't the voice of gloom," Griffin places a kiss on top of my head. "It's just... well, who you are."

"Oh lovely!" I say.

"That's not what I mean. It's just, when you are standing next to someone like the Professor, of course you are going to look more..."

I raise one eyebrow.

"Responsible," he finishes, and seems pleased with the word choice.

"You were next to him yesterday and you came off as carefree and vivacious," I say, thinking of his laughing face as the wind whipped through his hair.

"Don't tell me this is actually bothering you."

"Of course it is," I say, shaking my head. "I don't want everyone thinking I'm such a negative nelly."

"June, it's film. Everyone is miserable," Griffin says, and brings his lips to mine. "Just forget about it."

"I can't though," I shake my head. "It's ingrained in my head. I *wish* I could just forget things. I wish I could let them go. But... I can't."

I sigh and adjust the covers. I know how I can be. I know how other people think I am a little... anal. And I want to relax, I really do. Watching myself on the video I can see what Griffin and the Professor are on about at home. I *do* nag them. They all seem to be having a wonderful time, and there I am standing behind them and frowning. Or telling them to stop doing something. And my voice takes on this exasperated, high pitched tone that comes across as patronizing. After watching the latest video, I keep vowing that tomorrow I will be different, I'll let them get on with it and enjoy the experience. Obviously I would like to be more carefree. But then I have to wrestle a loaded pistol off a man with Alzheimer's, or I stub my toe on the typewriter he hasn't taken the cover off and my resolution goes out the window.

"June, you're a lovely, caring person," Griffin says brushing the hair back from my forehead.

"You don't think... I mean, you don't think I nag you a bit much. Or boss you around?" I peer up into his face.

"To be honest—and I'm only admitting this because you've clearly on the verge of a breakdown," he qualifies. "I kind of like it when you boss me around. I guess—I guess it reminds me that you care."

"Griffin," I say, putting my hand on his chest as he shrugs.

"You wouldn't bother if you didn't care," he puts his hand over mine.

"Of *course* I care," I look up into his eyes. "I love you."

"I know," he says, kissing me again while he leans across me to switch off the light.

Chapter Eleven

"Mum called me yesterday," Griffin says, indicating to change lanes as I grip the armrest between us.

"Hmm?" I ask, pushing my foot into the car's floor as we almost hit the car ahead of us.

"Keep forgetting the bloody pedals are the wrong way round," he looks down in frustration.

"Eyes on the road!" I yell.

"What?" he looks up. "I saw him."

I choose not to make a comment in case it distracts him further.

The Professor and Dr Cooke are in the back and are on their third rendition of a song they've come up with for the journey set to the tune of *The Yellow Brick Road*. Clint put headphones on about twenty minutes ago.

"We're here to find some treasure in the good old wild, wild west. It seems a shame without a gun, but June thinks that she knows best."

I frown, and try and block out the noise.

"So what did Ruth say?" I ask Griffin.

"No clue, didn't get to speak to her," Griffin frowns, shaking his head. "Pearl didn't think I was in."

"She can be a bit flighty," I say to him, putting my hand up to the ceiling as we take a turn a little too quickly.

"That old bat knows *exactly* what she's doing," Griffin says, braking rather forcefully. "You would think an automatic would be easier, but I miss my manual."

"Why would she not want you to speak with your mother?" I ask him, trying to hide my exasperation.

"No clue," Griffin says, indicating to move around a tractor on the road. "There's just something off about her, I can't put my finger on it."

Now I really do roll my eyes.

"Well, did you try calling her back?" I ask him.

"She wasn't home," Griffin says, shifting around in his seat. "But Pearl said she thought someone was there with my Mum."

"Who?" I ask in surprise. I've never heard Ruth speak about a single friend she has.

"I don't know," Griffin shakes his head. "It's not like her. She doesn't really like company, you know, with her nerves."

Luckily I'm saved from responding by the two men in the back belting out the last part of their song.

"Lacking an ounce of etiquette, in Good Old America."

The two of them burst into laughter at the end, and look to Clint for encouragement, but his eyelids are half closed in exasperation.

"What has gotten into you two?" I say, and can't help

but smile at their contagious laughter. "I thought you were dreading this car ride?"

"We were," Dr Cooke says and winks at the Professor.

The Professor leans forward in his seat and says in a mock whisper, "Pearl gave us a little something to help with the journey."

"What?" I ask, looking at the two of them for further explanation. "What do you mean? What did she give you?"

"Nothing," Dr Cooke gives the Professor a warning glance and puts his finger to his lips.

"What did she give you?" I ask again, staring at the Professor.

His eyes widen and suddenly he seems like a little boy who has been caught with his hand in the cookie jar.

"Just a bit of Marijuana," the Professor mumbles. "But, it was for medicinal purposes!"

"She *what?*" I yell, causing Griffin to swerve a bit to the right.

"What the hell!" Clint yells from beside them, pulling the headphones off his ears and setting them around his neck. "Anytime I've asked her, she says I need a prescription!"

"You *what?*" I yell at Clint, and I feel my face turning red with anger.

Clint shrinks back from my look and quickly replaces his headphones.

"June, it's fine," Dr Cooke tries to calm me, and I can

see his movements are a little slower than usual. "I don't think it really worked on us, to be honest. Bad batch."

"I feel no difference at all," the Professor tries to grab onto something imaginary in front of his face.

"I cannot believe this!" I say, shaking in outrage. "You are on a very strict plan with the doctor. Who knows what this will do to your medication! She could have *really* endangered you."

"She made us a cake," the Professor shrugs. "It seemed the polite thing to do was eat it."

"And you!" I say pointing to Dr Cooke. "How could you let him eat that? You know how serious his condition is!"

"June dear, you're overreacting," Dr Cooke blinks slowly at me. "We only had…"

I wait for him to finish, but he just keeps blinking at me.

"You only had what?" I ask him.

"What?" he frowns.

"You said, 'I only had…'," I prompt.

"Did I?" he asks, turning to the Professor.

"Don't remember," the Professor shrugs. "But that's nothing new."

Dr Cooke slaps his knee as the two of them howl in laughter. My lips thin and I turn around in my seat.

"I cannot *believe* this," I whisper to Griffin.

"Well…" Griffin's voice lingers.

"*Well*, what?" I turn my head to him.

"I did warn you…" He tries to keep his tone light, but I can see the vindication on his face.

"You warned me that Pearl was going to give illegal narcotics to my ill grandfather?" I say, directing some of my pent up rage at Griffin now.

"I tried to warn you about her," Griffin says, holding up his hand in defence. "I told you there was something off about her…"

I clench my jaw and decide not to answer.

"I'm going to *kill* her," I say, wanting to hit something.

It's just so dangerous what she did. It has taken us years to find the right balance of medication that seems to work for the Professor. His episodes have been reduced greatly over the past year, he has more energy, he's able to be more independent.

I look in the rear-view mirror. The two of them have starting humming their tune again.

He's fine right now, I assure myself. They are both fine. Maybe they didn't have very much; maybe it will start to wear off shortly and there won't be any side effects from it.

We pull into the small parking lot of the museum and the men file out of the car, and though the two older men look more relaxed and subdued I have to admit they don't seem particularly worse for wear from eating Pearl's cake.

If anything, they're very quiet now we are here and haven't mentioned anything to do with that bloody camera so maybe I should thank Pearl when I get home.

We walk onto the small rickety porch and look around. The front door has been left open, and there doesn't seem to be a sign of life inside.

I turn to look at the others.

"Do we just go in?" I ask.

Griffin shrugs beside me, and takes another look around.

"It's pretty secluded out here," he says. "They probably don't get many visitors."

"It's probably run by volunteers," I comment, poking my head through the front door. "These places usually are."

The inside looks like an old cabin. To the left is a large fireplace, not lit, which gives the room an abandoned feel. On the far right wall is a long wooden table with items displayed on the top. The wood floors look well worn and dirty in the centre, probably from where everyone usually walks on them. Straight ahead is a small doorway, which I assume leads to the kitchen, which was usually built at the back of the house. To the left is a small bedroom, the lumps in the bed visible through the dark red and green quilt on top. The back of the house is only a dozen paces from the front.

I feel a quick push on my back and stumble a little against the frame. Stepping back I turn around to see Clint's bright red face.

"Sorry, the camera was stuck in the bag... I think er—I might have... by accident," he stutters.

I'm actually quite enjoying how afraid he is of me, and if

he thinks I will forget about him uploading that video any time soon he's got another thing coming.

"Come on," I say to the others and take a step over the threshold.

Chapter Twelve

"Well hello there!" I hear a voice to my right and jump.

"Christ almighty!" I yell, and turn to see a man sitting just through the door on an old wooden chair. "I didn't see you there!"

"I've spent so much time in this old place I must be blending into the walls," the man laughs.

He's wearing a plaid shirt under a leather vest with corduroy pants. His thick black glasses seem much too big for his face and I notice he has the same habit as me of pushing them up the bridge of his nose.

"I'm George," he says, extending his hand.

"June, June Jenson," I return his smile.

I turn and make introductions of the others.

"Sorry, no photography or cameras in here," he says to Clint. "We ask people to view it the same way they would in the nineteenth century."

I see Clint roll his eyes as he puts the camcorder away in his bag.

"Right, well what brings you out here, June?" George asks.

"Well, we're archaeologists who are in the area studying

some remains which we believe may have belonged to Butch Cassidy," I say, looking around the room again. "And we thought what better place to get some more information than a museum dedicated to him?"

"You've come to the right place," George nods, placing his hands on his stomach. "Butch himself is believed to have visited this very home, which was owned by the Bassett family."

"May I?" I ask, pointing to the pictures on the wall.

"Of course, that's what it's here for," he says, and the others begin to disperse around the room. George, however, follows me.

The framed pictures on the wall are all ones I have seen before through the various history books in Oxford's library. Butch Cassidy in his famous group portrait of the Wild Bunch Gang, the picture of Etta Place who ran away with him and Harry Alonzo Longabaugh.

"This is Josie Bassett?" I ask, turning to George and pointing at the picture of a handsome older woman on the wall.

"About twenty years after Butch went to Argentina," he answers, nodding. "Most of the items here have been donated by the Bassett family. Do you know much about them?"

"Probably not nearly as much as you," I smile and hope to flatter him into telling me everything he knows.

As much as it pains me to admit, there's a lot of

information missing from history books, and what better way to get information than from a dedicated volunteer who probably knows Butch Cassidy's trouser size.

"Well, Herb Bassett owned a farm not too far from here and used to sell horses and beef to the outlaws. That's how Ann and Josie initially got mixed up in everything. They were both very attractive young women: well educated and skilled in horsemanship. Ann became involved with Butch Cassidy when she was fifteen years old," he says, and points to a picture of the woman history refers to as Queen Ann. "But Butch went to jail for rustling cattle, and Ann started stepping out with a man named Ben Kilpatrick."

"Josie took up with Butch after that, but things didn't last too long and they broke it off around the time Elzy Lay started courting Maude Davis," he explains.

"Who's Elzy Lay?" Griffin asks, coming to stand beside me.

"Who's Elzy Lay?" George asks, a laugh escaping his throat at the absurdity of the question.

"Griffin's not an archaeologist," I explain, and put my hand on his arm when Griffin looks like he's offended by George's reaction.

"Elzy Lay and Butch Cassidy are the creators of the Wild Bunch Gang—oh, er... that's a group of outlaws from the nineteenth century," he explains slowly to Griffin.

Griffin stares at George, then nods his thanks in mock appreciation.

"The two of them formed the gang at Robber's Roost, a cabin which was owned by Ann and Josie Bassett in Utah. The outlaws would use it to "lay low" after a robbery because it was next to impossible for someone to approach it without them seeing," George continues, turning from Griffin to me. "The only women ever known to be allowed in were the Bassett sisters, Etta Price, Maude Davis and the sole female gang member, Laura Billion. There was such secrecy to the location that in all the time Butch was an outlaw here in America not a single lawman knew the location of the hideout."

"Sounds like they were quite the groupies," Griffin offers, and I notice George bristles at the comment.

"Those women were vital to the Wild Bunch Gang. Keeping the law off of their trail, helping them hide some of the loot from robberies until they were able to return for it," he lists off.

"They helped him hide things?" I say, trying not to seem too enthusiastic at the news.

George narrows his eyes and looks between me and Griffin, setting his weight on his heels and crossing his arms across his chest.

"You're looking for the lost treasure," he finally says.

"Er—well, yes," I admit.

He shakes his head and lets out a soft chuckle. "You and every other treasure hunter that's come to Colorado for the last century. You'll never find it."

"We're not treasure hunters," I argue. "We are archaeologists."

"That's a very grey line now a days," he counters.

"Well, regardless, we are here for the *history*," I say.

"Well, if that's all you're here for, look no further," George says and spreads his arms out wide. "We've got an abundance."

"You said he was with Josie after he was let out of prison," I say, trying to get him back on track. "What happened then?"

"Well, not long after he called it off with her and took up with her sister Ann again," he says.

Griffin whistles. "That must have been some interesting family dinners."

"They all changed partners quite frequently," he waves off the comment.

Griffin rubs his nose in an attempt to hide his grin.

"Then there was the big train robbery and Butch left for South America, leaving Josie and the remaining members of the Wild Bunch Gang in America."

"And Ann," I add.

"Maybe," George says, his mouth lifting at one side before he leans in and whispers, "Some people think her and Etta Price are one in the same, and she went to South America with Cassidy and the Sundance Kid."

"That's sounds more like a conspiracy theorists idea," I say to him.

He stands up straight again and nods. "Not likely, sure. But you never really can tell with Butch Cassidy what's fact and what's legend."

"So Josie lived around here until she passed?" I ask him.

"Oh yeah, the old bat got crazier with age. Constantly claiming Butch died an old man in Utah and visited her frequently. Not one person could back up her story, but that's half the fun of it, isn't it?" he asks, wiggling his eyebrows.

"What do you mean?" I ask.

"Well no one could prove she was lying, either," he says, and I let his words sink in for a moment.

"What's this?" I ask, pointing to a large map on the wall.

"Oh, this is a survey old Josie drew of one of her family's properties," he says. "They owned multiple..."

I turn to look at Dr Cooke who's materialized at my side, his eyes studying the map.

"Does it look..." Dr Cooke says, his brow furrowed.

"It's Pearl's property," I say under my breath in confirmation.

"What's that?" George asks, not catching my words.

"I was just admiring it," I say quickly.

What does this mean? My mind races as I study the weathered paper with the black ink faded almost to blue.

"It is one of our more recent acquisitions. I believe it was found in Josie's attic not long ago when the family decided to sell the farm house she lived in until she died," he says.

"Did the Bassett family own a lot of property in this area, or was it spread out around the state?" I ask him.

"Mainly in this area," he says. "Of course it was severed many times because men would come…"

I nod as he drones on about another history lesson. It could be a coincidence. Pearl's place isn't far from here, so it only makes sense that if the Bassetts owned a lot of the area, Pearl's property would be included in that. It just seems like fate, the land survey hanging on the wall here. It seems like it is calling out to me, but I don't know what it's saying.

"Those loopy W's are to indicate the wells on the property. See there," he points to one in the middle of small peaks which Josie must have drawn to indicate the forest we have ridden through so often the past week. "And another next to this mountain area."

"Josie must have been indicating water sources," I point to the top part of the map that is torn, but the loopy W is still visible on the edge. "That's actually a stream."

"You've been there?" George asks, turning to look at me with interest.

"Er—yes," I say.

"You can see the original farm house marked on it, and the acres of agricultural land," he points out.

"Do you know if Cassidy ever stayed there?" I ask him.

"Oh, I suspect they all rode through there at some point…."

I nod.

"June!" the Professor's eager voice calls me and I turn to see him with Clint by the sideboard on the far wall.

I walk over quickly, not seeing a small wooden stool in my path and tripping over it, falling into a heap on the old wooden floor.

Griffin puts his hand under my arm to help me up, and I push my glasses up as my face flames red.

"What is it?" I ask the Professor when I reach him and follow his gaze down to the table in front of us.

I gasp when I see a small gilded picture frame on the sideboard. I squint and study every inch of the small photograph.

"That's an old picture of Robber's Roost," George explains, coming up behind us.

I turn to look at Dr Cooke, who has brought his hand up to cover his mouth.

The photograph is sepia in colour, the colour of almost every photograph from before the 1950's when multi-coloured photographs became more common. The photographer captured a small sitting area, not much bigger then the one we stand in now. A large table sits off to the left side, and I can only imagine the discussions that must have occurred with the Wild Bunch Gang gathered around it. To the right is a small chair and a wooden bench on the edge of a worn rug in front of the fireplace's hearth. The fireplace has no flame but a pile of logs sit beside it. On the mantle are two dark wooden candlesticks with a farmland painting hanging above. And in the centre of the mantle sits a little wooden box with three gold interlocking rings embedded in the front.

"Is this stuff still there in Robber's Roost?" I ask George. The sense of eagerness and excitement seems to be palpable in the air from our entire group.

"No, most of it was cleared out long ago," he answers, shaking his head. "The Bassett family probably took it before the place closed up."

"This box," I say, pointing to the mantle in the photograph. "Have you ever seen it at another museum? Do you know if the family still has it?"

He shakes his head again. "No, they don't."

"You know for certain?" I ask him.

"Yes, the family searched for it when they found the photograph after Josie passed, but it never turned up. They thought it most likely belonged to Cassidy," he shrugs, and then sees us exchanging glances with each other. "Why? Is it important or something?"

I turn to look at him, trying to tamp down the excitement coursing through me.

"I'd bet my bonnet it's the key to everything."

Chapter Thirteen

I'm on such a euphoric high that when we get back to the ranch I don't realize there are a half dozen vehicles parked out front until I bump right into one.

I look around, frowning.

"Pearl must have guests," Griffin suggests.

"Maybe she's having a narcotics party," the Professor says, looking at the white, unmarked vans in front of her house. "We might finally be able to get a hot cup of tea if she's entertaining."

"Umm—" I say, slowly walking to the house as my heart feels like it is suddenly lodged in my throat. "I don't think—"

Before I am able to finish my thought the front door opens and I think I might sink to my knees.

Phillip Hurst strolls out the front door, looking unbelievably smug, with a deep set tan and his perfect wavy hair.

"June," he says, his face splitting into a broad smile. "It's so good to see you again."

"I—" I start, but can't seem to speak at the moment.

"I can't say I really expected to be meeting you here," he

says, "But any chance to see you is surely a pleasure."

He turns his head in the direction of Pearl and the other people who have followed him out of the house. I notice, to my chagrin, that a lot of the people Phillip has decided to bring are students from the University. They are about to see me in all of my glory.

Phillip flashes a smile at Pearl, who I'm surprised to see is resistant to its charming potency.

"I—" I start again, but am quickly cut off by the Professor.

"Now, see here, what's all of this about?" he pushes past me.

"Sir, I am Professor Phillip Hurst, and I am here on behalf of Oxford University about Butch Cassidy's lost treasure," he says, turning his charm on the Professor.

The Professor visibly relaxes and nods his head. "Good, the University has finally seen fit to send us some help."

"They have," Phillip smiles indulgently.

Dr Cooke walks forward at this news.

"Well, I think it best to establish right off who's in charge," Dr Cooke says, and places his hand on the Professor's shoulder.

"That's the first thing I intend to do," Phillip nods, his eyes darting back to me.

"Phillip, they had nothing to do with this," I step forward.

"Like hell we didn't!" the Professor argues, straightening

his hat. "We are just as much responsible for all of this as you are."

"Can you please just let me handle this," I say through gritted teeth.

"Sir, I am from the American Historical Society," an older man standing behind Phillip steps forward and removes his hat. "Who exactly are you?"

"Who am I?" the Professor says, standing up straighter. "I am Professor Albert Arthur Jenson, formally Head of the Oxford University Archaeology Department, and currently working on an important assignment from her majesty's Association of British Archaeology."

"And I'm Dr Daniel Cooke—" Dr Cooke starts but is cut off by Phillip.

"June, perhaps it would be best for your... er... *colleagues* to wait inside," Phillip suggests, nodding to the man beside him. "Then we can all have a little chat and get this sorted."

I breathe in deeply at his condescending tone, but admit that in this particular case he might be right.

"Now, just you wait a minute—we're not going anywhere!" Griffin yells and gallantly steps in front of me.

There are times that the gesture is sweet, but in this particular case I wish he would stay out of it.

Phillips smile widens slightly, but he makes no further comment. Of course he wants them to witness my full humiliation and he's somehow coming off as the gentlemen.

"June, may I ask what you are doing in Colorado?"

Phillip says, placing one hand across his chest and the other on his chin.

"What do you mean, what is she doing here?" Griffin laughs at him before turning to me. "What's this idiot going on about?"

"I—" I shake my head, willing Griffin to say no more.

"I must say the University was very distressed to learn you had come here," Phillip continues. "At first I tried to assure them you must be trying to get a head start on the background work for me— I've always appreciated your efforts on the detailed reports you've written for me. But then they saw the videos on the Internet, and well... June I must say, I saw them and well, it didn't look like you were only researching."

Phillip sighs as though disappointed.

The smug bastard.

"What videos?" I say, but whirl my head to stare at Clint.

"I—er... I didn't actually take the video down," he mumbles, lowering his eyes to the ground. "They were getting such great views."

"*They?*" I force out through my clenched teeth.

"Well, when I saw how many people were watching the first one, I uploaded a few more of them," he says, looking anywhere but at me. "We are up to nearly twenty thousand followers."

"How many videos?" I ask, my hands fisted at my sides.

"All of them," he mumbles.

I lunge at him, and Griffin catches me around my waist.

"Stop it!" Griffin tells me.

"We're famous," the Professor says in wonder, looking at Dr Cooke.

"Really June, I had thought you knew or I never would have…" I can hear the glee in Phillip's voice.

"Would you just shut up for a minute!" Griffin yells at him before turning to me again. "June, what is going on?"

"I—" I say, searching his face.

The look of concern on his face crushes me. I so wish he would be angry instead.

"I lied to you," I whisper. "This isn't my excavation site. Oxford gave it to Phillip."

Griffin frowns. "But Oxford assigned this to you," he shakes his head. "How else did you get them to agree…"

"I lied to them too," I say, forcing myself to look at him and not at the ground. "I told them to give me the details of the site because I would do some preliminary research."

"Well, I'm just happy to be able to be of service," Phillip shrugs to the man beside him, but Griffin holds his finger up to silence him.

"And the Historical Society? How did you get them to agree to let you come?" Griffin looks around him. "How did you get them to pay for you to be here?"

"I—er, lied to them too." I say fidgeting with the hem of my sweater. "I told them I was coming to make sure everything was set up properly for Phillip."

"June Bug," the Professor shakes his head.

"I'm sorry. I'm so sorry I lied to you all," I say, looking at Griffin, who looks so disappointed. "I thought it was the only way I would ever get a site of my own—"

"You know, on my soul searching through the Congo Jungle I learned the word *bumósi*, which translates to sequestered peace," Phillip says, raising his eyebrows in thought. "I think it is appropriate for this situation. A little food for thought."

We all look at him, frowning, before I turn back to Griffin.

"Well, I'm afraid you will all have to leave immediately," the man from the Historical Society says, stepping forward. "I can't begin to tell you the legal ramifications of this deception–"

"Now, wait just a minute!" Dr Cooke yells from behind me. "We've done all the hard work and found out—"

I step on his foot quickly to silence him, but I notice that Phillip's interest has been piqued.

"Now, now, there is no reason to get hostile about this," Phillip says, taking a step forward. "There has to be some solution which will make everyone happy."

He turns to the man from the Historical Society and waits for his nod of approval. The man looks confused, but nods for Phillip to go on.

"Now June, I can't say Oxford is happy about this. Obviously I tried to smooth things over for you as best as I could before I left—"

"I bet you bloody did," I mutter under my breath.

"But, I can't say my opinion holds all the weight in the matter," he shrugs reluctantly. "However, if you were to help us out by telling us what you've found out so far, I can probably convince them not to fire you. And of course, the Historical Society wouldn't press charges."

"Charges? Charges for what?" I argue.

"Well, off the top of my head... Trespassing, accepting funding under false pretences..." Phillip pauses to let it sink in.

Yes I'm sure he's thought long and hard about all the trouble I am in.

"I didn't accept any money from anyone," I raise my chin defiantly.

"I believe the American Historical Society did fund your travel expenses, Ms Jenson," the man beside Phillip points out.

"I never deposited your cheque," I say, pulling my knapsack off of my back and opening it. "I have it right here, you can have it back!"

"Nevertheless," he says waving away the offered cheque in my hand. "You have trespassed under false pretences on private property—"

"No she ain't," Pearl says, sidling up beside me. "I invited her here."

"What? No you didn't!" Phillip yells, momentarily

forgetting about his pretences. When Pearl recoils he straightens his jacket and offers her a smile. "My dear Ms Pearl—"

"Don't you Ms Pearl me," she says, snatching her hand back after Phillip takes it between his own. "Miss June is here as my guest."

Phillip looks as though his patience might be fading.

"Well, whether she is here as your... *guest*... or not," he says, "You have a contract with the American Historical Society to dig up your land in order to find the coins."

"Yes, and the American Historical Society," the man tips his hat in the direction of Pearl, "chooses who will perform the excavation."

"They chose me," Phillip sighs as though it is a burden he is reluctantly taking on.

"And we have the full right to enforce the contract and submit to the authorities anyone who is trying to breach the contract," the man says, straightening his suit jacket.

I feel Pearl stand up straighter next to me, not missing the man's threat.

"That damn contract don't start until the fifteenth of September," Pearl says, spitting on the ground beside her.

"Ugh," the Professor cringes as the spittle lands next to his foot.

"And if my mind don't need adjusting, I do believe I am correct in believing it only to be the eighth of September."

"She's saying—" Clint whispers in the Professor's ear.

"Sshh!" the Professor hisses with his finger raised for silence, his eyes riveted on Pearl.

"Which means, you can just get the hell off of my property!" She says to Phillip, looping her arm through mine.

I feel a sudden need to kiss this woman profusely, but my eyes stay glued to Phillip, watching for his reaction.

His eyes narrow into slits as he stares at Pearl.

"You can't cancel the contract," he says.

"Who said anything about cancelling it?" Pearl shrugs at him.

"She can't be a part of it—the American Historical Society dictates—" he starts.

"You go dictate all you want—" Pearl clicks her tongue. "But June is staying as my guest for as long as she damn well pleases."

"And we've already claimed the bunk house, so don't get any notions about that!" Dr Cooke says, the Professor nodding in agreement.

"This is ridiculous," Phillip says to the man from the Historical Society. "Do something."

"Well, Ms Pearl is welcome to have any guests she wants, I suppose," he says, scratching his head. "And Ms Jenson didn't deposit the funds... Of course, your University can seek whatever disciplinary action they choose and Ms Jenson will not be taking part in our excavation."

Phillip turns to look at me and I raise my chin.

I'm not really sure why, obviously I won't be staying now

that I can't be a part of the excavation.

We were *so* close though.

"Fine," Phillip says, trying to shrug off his annoyance. "Stay. In fact, by all means, stay and watch as we uncover the treasure. You will probably learn a lot."

I will myself to remain composed as he leans closer to me. Our faces are almost touching. "I think I would quite enjoy that," he whispers.

I'm proud to say I give away nothing, though I am seething inside.

He straightens and turns to the people behind him.

"Come, we can go to the hotel and prepare ourselves for the discovery of our careers."

I clench my teeth as the people start filing past us towards their cars.

"Of course, if June here were to find the treasure before the fifteenth you won't need to return," Pearl says so low I think I might be the only one who heard her.

"What?" Phillip whirls round.

Okay, so I wasn't the only one.

"Well," Pearl shrugs. "That contract starts on the fifteenth, and this is my property… if June finds it before the fifteenth then the discovery is hers, ain't that right?"

"That's right," Dr Cooke says, catching on. "If we find the coins before the contract commences then by the laws of this God forsaken land, it's 'finders keepers', so the treasure belongs to Pearl and the discovery belongs to June."

"Well, what are we waiting for!" Clint yells from besides me and I jump. I had forgotten he was there.

"Now wait just a minute—you can't—" Phillip looks to the man from the Historical Society who looks like he just swallowed something disgusting.

"Well, *technically...*" he doesn't finish his sentence.

"It doesn't matter," Phillip shrugs away the notion, shaking his head. "There is not a chance in hell you will find that treasure in seven days."

"I guess we'll see, won't we?" I raise an eyebrow at him.

He stares at me for a moment, and I can see he believes he underestimated me. If I didn't know him better, I would almost say he was impressed. But he says nothing and turns to get in the car, slamming the door shut.

Oh God, what have I done?

Pearl squeezes my arm in encouragement as we watch the cars peel out of her driveway, leaving a cloud of dust in their wake.

"Oh God," I say, bending over and clutching my stomach as the last car disappears. "What have I done?"

"Never mind that now," the Professor says, pulling out his journal. "We have seven days to find this bloody treasure and all we know now is what the blasted box that the bloody key goes with looks like. We don't even know if the coins are in it!"

"They have to be Albert," Dr Cooke emphatically proclaims. "It all adds up. We found the key in the exact same spot as the coin—we're academics Albert, we know these sort of things don't just happen by coincidence. Whoever buried that coin wanted the person to find the key as well. It's a *clue*."

"But we still don't know where the box could be," I argue.

"Then we've missed something," the Professor grasps his chin in deep concentration. "We know the who, the what, the when, and the how. But what is the *where*?"

"I say we go back to that tree tomorrow, and we don't come back until we know the location of the box," Dr Cooke adds.

I look at their serious, determined faces and have to smile.

"Listen, I owe you all an apology, I never should have put you at risk like this—" I begin.

"Save the I'm sorrys for after we find the treasure," the Professor says, making notes in his journal.

"Wow, I never thought you two would be the optimists of the group," I say looking at their eager faces. "Okay, let's do it."

Dr Cooke claps his hands together in excitement.

"What do you think, Griffin?" I turn to look at him but he's striding back to the house. I jump as he slams the door behind him.

Chapter Fourteen

"He won't speak to me," I say to Clint as we come through the clearing at the end of the forest. "I've tried everything!"

He nods non-committedly as he has done for most of the ride.

"It's because I lied to him," I tell Clint for the dozenth time. "You think it's that, right?"

He shrugs.

"I heard him trying to call his mother all evening," I say, shaking my head. "What do you think I should do?"

He shrugs again.

"Well, you've just been so helpful, considering this is all your fault!" I snap at him as we dismount from our horses.

"*My fault?*" he says, turning to me.

"If you had just taken down those bloody videos like I told you to none of us would be in this mess," I argue.

"Yeah, because you lying to everyone wasn't the issue…" he says, raising his eyebrows.

"Well if you hadn't broadcast to the world what we were doing, no one would have ever known," I counter.

"If it weren't for me we wouldn't be a YouTube

sensation, right now," Clint points out. "So maybe you should chill out a bit."

I narrow my eyes at him, and take a step forward.

"Oh leave the poor boy alone, June Bug," the Professor lands on the ground ever so gracefully as Dr Cooke falls off of his horse. "It's not his fault you've gone and fuddled everything up again."

"Lovely, thanks for the support," I say, tying my horse to the nearby tree.

"There was a lot of slamming doors yesterday, wasn't there?" Dr Cooke looks concerned at me. "Still getting the silent treatment?"

"He won't even look at me," I say, shaking my head. "I mean, I know what I did was wrong…"

"Terrible," the Professor nods in agreement.

"But I was trying to protect you all. I mean, it's not something I was *proud* of," I say in my defence. The Professor and Dr Cooke nod in agreement, but Clint raises his eyebrows, not convinced.

I choose to ignore him.

"I mean, you both forgave me right?"

"I can't even remember what you did, to be honest," the Professor shrugs jovially.

"And you could have been in a lot of trouble with your internship thing…" I continue.

Dr Cooke's eyes widen.

"I'd never thought of that—my God, what if they cut

our funding? What if we have to give him back?" he says, pointing to Clint. "And now with all our fans, who will answer our post?"

"Oh, I'm sure they won't mind…" I start.

"We only got him because we told them about this dig…" Dr Cooke bites his fingernail in earnest looking at the Professor. "What do you think, Albert?"

"Well, he's not going back!" the Professor says, going to stand next to Clint. "He's ours, we found him first. And he's the only one who knows the password to upload our videos."

I look at Clint, who seems a bit dazed by the two men.

"Look at him, he'd be lost without us now," the Professor says, patting him gently on the head. "Wouldn't you, Carl?"

"Er—I think I'd be okay…"

"Poor thing," the Professor ruffles Clint's hair and turns to Dr Cooke.

"Everything should be alright if we find the coins," Dr Cooke says, more to himself than anyone. "Surely they wouldn't take him back if we find them…"

"So, it's settled then," I say to them all. "We just have to find the coins in seven days—"

"Six now," Clint says, sidestepping the Professor's outstretched hand.

"Right, six days, or we are all seriously buggered," I say, with a forced nod.

"I've been in worse," the Professor says, his eyes a little glazed. "Why, when Liberty Valance had poor Ransom squared at the end of his barrel, I pulled my Winchester out and—"

"Oh wonderful, bloody John Wayne is back," Dr Cooke mutters as the Professor mimes the actions to taking out his imaginary foe.

Dr Cooke and I collect our small bag of tools from the saddlebags of his horse and make our way over to the excavation area while Clint tries to fend off the Professor's swiping hands.

"It wouldn't be any deeper," I say, looking down at the exposed earth. "Unless it got past us and is in the dirt pile."

"We combed through it all—I'm sure of it," Dr Cooke assures me, though he eyes the pile in question.

"We've dug four feet past where we found the coin—there's not a chance he would have buried anything deeper than that," I argue. "This just doesn't make any sense. Do you think he left the clues with Josie Bassett?"

"The family never saw a box, they thought it belonged to Butch. Maybe he left her with the clues for the treasure in case he couldn't return from South America, though," Dr Cooke scratches his head.

"But, where is it?" I say, looking around hopelessly. "Where are the *clues*?"

"Perhaps we missed something at the museum," Dr Cooke suggests.

"We saw every inch of that place. I've gone over it in my mind and there's nothing…" I say in frustration.

"It all hinges on that box—I can just feel it. But how do we find it?" Dr Cooke looks back into the hole as though the box will miraculously appear.

"If Butch buried the treasure in the chest then it must be somewhere between the train and Robber's Roost," I argue. "He wasn't likely to carry that big chest with him to the robbery, so he must have robbed the train and brought the coins to a prearranged spot and buried them in the chest. The Pinkerton Detective Agency was right on his heels after the robbery. He wouldn't have wanted to divert his course for risk of not being able to get to the hide out before being caught."

"Once they were at the hide out it was all but impossible to find them," Dr Cooke nods in agreement. "And this is right on course between the hideout and the train."

"So where's the bloody treasure then?" I say, throwing down my spade.

Dr Cooke sighs. "No clue, June. Not a bloody one."

Chapter Fifteen

Covered in grime from the ride I decide it's best if I take a quick shower. I walk into the bedroom and stop in my tracks as Griffin throws a shirt into his overflowing suitcase.

"What are you doing?" I frown.

He looks up at me, the anger evident on his face.

"What does it look like?" he asks.

"It… it looks like you're packing," I say, taking a tentative step towards him. "Where are you going?"

"Home," he says, snapping the lid of the suitcase down.

"What? Why?" I lift my hand to put it on his shoulder, but pull it back as I see his jaw clenching.

He doesn't say anything, but pulls the zipper closed on his suitcase.

"Griffin, I'm sorry!" I say, trying to force my face into his line of sight. "I don't know what else to say, you won't talk to me!"

He snorts, shaking his head. "Now I guess you know how it feels," he says.

"Griffin, please," I say, holding onto the sleeve of his shirt. "I didn't mean to hurt you, I was trying to protect you."

"No you weren't," he says, pulling his sleeve free from

my grasp. "You were trying to protect *yourself*."

I recoil from the rebuke.

"How can you say that? I— "

"I can say it, because it's *true,*" he says, and pushes past me to get to the dresser where his watch is sitting on the top.

"I—I can't believe you think that," I say, trying not to let the hurt in my voice come through.

He stops at the dresser and places both hands on the top, his head bowed between them.

"You don't trust me, June," he says, shaking his head. "How can we be in a relationship when you don't even *trust* me."

"I do—" I start, but he cuts me off.

"No you don't," he says so quietly I have to strain to catch his words. "This whole thing had nothing to do with me. The Professor and Dr Cooke—I can see why you kept this from them. But why me?"

I open my mouth to answer but nothing comes out. The truth is, I don't know. I don't know why I couldn't tell Griffin, why I couldn't include him. He would have gone along with it—I know he would have. He would have thought it was crazy, he would have argued, and told me I was insane. But he would have helped me. He would have done anything I needed to make it work. But I couldn't tell him, and I don't know why.

"I wanted to tell you, but then you kept saying all those lovely things about me, how I deserved this," my voice cracks. "I couldn't tell you after that."

"So this is *my* fault?" he says, putting his hand to his chest.

"No, of course not. It's just… I just wanted you to be proud of me," I say, playing with the hem of my sweater as I fight back the tears.

"I don't need you to be a famous archaeologist to be proud of you, June," Griffin says. "But for some reason you need that to be proud of yourself."

I open my mouth to argue, but nothing comes out because I don't know what to say.

"Christ, did you even think about the Professor and Dr Cooke?" he argues, running his hand through his hair in frustration. "You dragged them into this—"

"I didn't want them to come!" I cut him off. "They basically forced me to let them come."

Even as I say the words I know how hollow they are.

"Damn it June, you know what those two are like! What is this going to do to them if someone goes to the press?" Griffin shakes his head. "The Professor survived before because he knew he hadn't done anything wrong—can you argue you haven't done what they are accusing you of this time?"

A tear falls over my lashes as I look at him with shame.

"How did you think this was going to turn out, June?" Griffin asks.

"I just thought if I could find the coins, then everything

would be alright. Oxford would see I can do this *and* be a Professor–"

"And this is the way you convince them?" he asks in utter confusion. "You thought you would just go home and everything would be okay?"

"I just—I didn't know another way," I shrug hopelessly. "I've done everything they asked me to do, but they were never going to change their mind."

"Well, I hope it works out for you," he says.

"So, that's it? I make one mistake and you're leaving?" I ask him.

"June, this is one massive mistake," Griffin explains as though I am not grasping the gravity of the situation. "You lied to everyone. You lied to *me*. And I'm just supposed to say I forgive you?"

"Everyone else has," I say, throwing my arms up.

"Well I guess I am the one who can't," he says, picking up his jacket. "I don't know if it even matters to you anymore, but someone should show you there are consequences for your actions."

"Oh, and you are just the master of responsibility!" I yell at him. "How's that screenplay coming along? And, how did your Mum take it when you told her she wasn't moving in with us?"

"That is not the same thing," Griffin argues.

"Maybe not, but it's pretty damn close."

"I know I don't have a lot of things in my life together,"

he says, finally meeting my eyes. "When you met me I lived with my mother, was driving a taxi to make ends meet, and not doing much with my life. But that was my life. It was my comfort. And then I met you, and all of a sudden I wanted to do things for myself that I've never wanted before. And I wanted them with you.

"I know it seems like I didn't have to give up much, there wasn't much there to begin with. But June, I changed my life to be with you. But you have never, even tried to change your life to be with me," he says. "All I've heard since last year is how horrible everything in your life is. How nothing is going your way and other people are getting what you deserve. And I'm sick of it. And the thing is you do deserve the best. You deserve this opportunity more than anyone. The way you care for the Professor, and for me—I mean you even put up with Mum. But just know that while you aren't getting everything you want in life, the rest of us aren't either. I've changed who I am to be with you, but you can't give up your tightly held control for even a second. That's why you didn't tell me what was going on. You didn't trust me not to do exactly what you had planned. You were so afraid that if you told me that I would somehow mess it all up for you!"

"Griffin, that not true," I cry out.

"You know what? I think that deep down you like that the Professor isn't well. This way you can control him like you control everything else in life," he shakes his head. "Well, I'm sorry June, but I'm not going to let you control me anymore.   I want to be your partner, not your submissive."

"I… I think I was embarrassed," I say, my voice shaking. "You have your play, and the screenplay, and I—I have nothing."

Griffin sighs before standing up straight. He turns to look at me with pity in his eyes.

"If you really think that, I guess it doesn't matter if I stay, or if I go." He walks past me and picks up his suitcase before I even have time to register the action.

I turn to see him pulling the door open and walking out into the hall. I want to call after him and tell him to stop, but I don't. Instead, I push the rim of my glasses up the bridge of my nose and sink onto the bed.

I didn't tell him because I didn't *want* to tell him, I realise. When you are in a committed relationship shouldn't you want to tell each other everything—good or bad? I look up at the empty doorway and feel just as hollow inside.

Chapter Sixteen

"So, he hasn't called then?" I say into the receiver, my mind running through the possibilities.

"No..." Ruth says, and I can hear the suspicion in her voice. "Is something wrong? Is Griffin there with you now?"

My eyes look up to the ceiling, and I try to tamp down my frustration.

Why in the name of God if he was here with me now, would I be calling you? I want to scream into the receiver.

"No, no, everything's fine," I assure her as the Professor and Dr Cooke enter the room.

I put my finger to my lips, indicating that I'm on the phone but they ignore me and keep chatting loudly.

"Who's that? Is that Griffin?" she asks.

"No, that's the Professor and Dr Cooke. Griffin is still—er—out."

I hear a noise on the phone which I'm not sure I appreciate.

"I've called three times a day, for the past six days and every time I do my son is not there. I need to speak to him; I want to know he's alright."

Quite frankly I have no reason to be upset because I haven't a clue where her son is at this moment—or where he's been all week.

After Griffin left, I was going to give him time to get home before I called him. But the next morning Ruth called looking for him, so I knew he wasn't back at home yet. And after the first few tries she's sunk her teeth into the idea that her not being able to get a hold of him is a bad sign. I happen to agree with her, but of course I'd never tell her that.

I mean, where is he? Is he in England? I tried to call the airline but they wouldn't tell me anything for security reasons—wankers.

I almost hope he is in England and not driving around America somewhere—I mean, I have been the passenger in the car while he's driving here and know he could full well be crashed in a ditch somewhere.

"He's fine, I'm taking very good care of him," I say, crossing my fingers behind my back. I actually feel terrible about lying to her—well, maybe not terrible. I mean the fact that she forced her son to let her move in with us less than a month ago is still pretty fresh in my mind. But I do feel bad. Somewhat.

"The thing is, I think Griffin heard Rupert in the room the last time we spoke," Ruth says.

"Who's Rupert?" I ask.

"He's… well…" Ruth says and I can just imagine her twirling the cord of the phone round her finger in a nervous gesture. "He's my boyfriend."

"Your *boyfriend*?" I ask in disbelief. "Does Griffin know?"

"I haven't been able to tell him yet," she cries. "It's just—just because I've taken a lover—"

Oh God.

"I don't want him to think he's any less important to me," she says, and I can hear the worry in her voice. "Nothing will change!"

"Well, maybe *some* things should change," I say in an offhand tone.

"Rupert won't replace his father," she tells me. "But, June, I'm a woman. I have needs. Needs which haven't been met in a very long time."

I stand still, the receiver clutched in my hand and pray that is as far as this conversation will go.

"Rupert's a plumber, so he's very good with his hands."

"Right, someone's just come through the door Ruth, I better just–"

"Is it Griffin?" she cuts me off.

"No—it's er…" I say, frowning. "Someone else."

"I want you to have him call me the minute he gets back!" she says as I slowly start to lower my face to the phone's base.

"I promise," I say, nodding to the air as I replace the receiver.

I stand up and sigh.

"No luck with the lad, then?" Dr Cooke says as the men sit down around the table scattered with all of our paperwork.

"I just want to know he's okay," I say, collapsing into the chair beside the Professor. "What if something happened to him?"

"I'm sure he's fine," the Professor waves off my worry. "He's probably holed up in a lovely little motel making his way through the mini fridge. At least, that's what I would be doing if I had been betrayed on every level."

I scowl at him. "That's what you would do if it were a Monday," I snap.

"Back to your corners you two," Dr Cooke says, picking up one of the papers. "We need to work this all out, and you two arguing isn't going to help."

"You're right, Daniel," the Professor says, picking up a survey of the land.

"Where's Clint with his bloody recording device when you need him?" Dr Cooke says.

"He's taking a nap. This morning took a lot out of him," The Professor explains.

"Yes, I'm sure it was very taxing on all of you watching me dig all of those holes," I snap.

"It's a lot for Clive to hold that camera up all day long," the Professor says. "Poor lad's wrist is quite sore."

"This is hopeless, we have..." I look down at the watch on my wrist. "Eighteen hours before we have to turn everything over."

"Turn everything over?" Dr Cooke lifts his gaze from the paper he was studying.

"I don't know," I say, shaking my head. "Even if I can't be the one to find it, it deserves to be found, right?"

"I'll have no more talk of turning anything over! Where's your fighting spirit?" the Professor asks in reproach.

"It left three hours ago when I fell off that godforsaken horse," I say, dropping my head to the desk.

"Okay, let's go over it again. What do we *know*?" Dr Cooke asks.

"Well, I lied to my work to get on a project that was never assigned to me in the first place, so I'm probably fired. I might be facing some sort of legal ramifications for lying to the Americans for breach of contract. And my boyfriend, who probably won't ever forgive me for lying to him, is missing somewhere in America and could be dead for all we know!" I break off in a sob, shaking my head.

Dr Cooke lightly pats my arm. "That's a shame dear, but I was referring to the coins."

"The original coin was found by the tree, here," the Professor says, pointing to the area on the map by the stream where we have been digging. "As well as the key."

"We've searched that whole area," I shake my head. "I can't dig any more holes—there's nothing else there. "

"It just doesn't make sense," Dr Cooke shakes his head. "The whole point of hiding treasure is to be able to find it again."

"Maybe Cassidy wanted to be the only person who could find it. Maybe he left the key and the coin there as a marker, but didn't need to leave the other clues because he knew where the actual treasure was," I say.

"No, that's not how it was done, June," the Professor shakes his head. "There was always a back up plan in case they couldn't come back and needed to tell someone else how to get the treasure."

"Maybe the boundary lines have changed—" Dr Cooke says, taking the survey from the Professor.

"No, Josie Bassett's map had the same property lines, as the one you're holding. If it was different in the nineteenth century her map would have been different.

"Well, maybe the river beside the tree wasn't that deep back then. There were two wells on the map in Bassett's house, so obviously the water from the stream was not enough to sustain the people who lived on the land. What if the stream has filled from the water running down the mountain and has covered where he buried the treasure," Dr Cooke says, gaining some excitement from the notion.

I shake my head. "If Cassidy was going to bury them that close, why wouldn't he just bury it all together?" I say, shaking my head.

"Why did they have two wells to support less than a dozen people and livestock?" the Professor says, obviously taking a liking to the idea. "Who knows what goes through these bloody American's minds?"

"That is odd," I agree, looking down at the map in front of me, but seeing Josie Bassett's map in my mind. "It's a lot of work to dig a well. Why would they when they have a natural source of water from the stream half a kilometre away?"

I frown in thought. I mean, nowadays people have multiple bathrooms in their home, but back then they wouldn't think twice about walking that distance to get water, especially considering what was involved in digging a well.

"Maybe they had a little hut close to the well—almost a hideaway," Dr Cooke says, sitting up straight.

"There was nothing on Bassett's map that showed a small building," I shake my head.

"Well, if it was where Cassidy hid sometimes, they wouldn't likely want to advertise it," Dr Cooke argues.

"I don't know, we've ridden through the forest so many times, I've never seen any indication of a building," I frown in concentration. "Maybe the well was there before they settled on the land, before the stream was formed and they just decided to mark it on the map for reference."

"If only she'd put the treasure on that bloody map!" the Professor slams down the paper in outrage. "She's put everything else on it! Backwards bloody country– don't know their ass from their elbows."

I look at him without seeing anything as my mind grasps onto a small possibility.

"What did you say?" I ask him.

"Sorry, it's just since we've come to this blasted country I've not had a proper cup of tea and it's infuriating!" the Professor shakes his head.

"No, about the map," I say, and turn to look at Dr Cooke. "What if we have been looking at this whole thing *backwards*."

"What do you mean?" he frowns at me.

"We've been digging for the coins and the key, hoping they would lead us to some sort of map to the treasure. But what if we found the things on the map, without knowing it," I say, reaching for the survey again.

"I'm not sure I follow," Dr Cooke shakes his head.

"We are assuming that the key and the coin will point us in some sort of direction to the treasure—we've been viewing them as our map. What if we've found the clues *without* the map," I say, standing up in excitement.

The Professor looks at Dr Cooke. "I think she might have dug one too many holes today…"

"No, this makes sense," I say, waving off his words. "The reason we haven't got a clue where the treasure is, is because we've only found the secondary clues, and Cassidy must have assumed that if you found the clues then you would know where the treasure was already and needed the key to open it."

"How?" Dr Cooke frowns.

"Because you would have had the map!" I say, rooting

through the papers to find the picture of the coin and key. "We found them by chance."

"That's all well and good June, but we don't have the map," the Professor reminds me.

"Yes, we do," I say, slapping down the survey of the land.

"Er—Are we missing something? Dr Cooke says, peering over at the paper.

"No, this is," I say, pointing my finger at it. "It doesn't have Josie Bassett's markers on it."

"About the wells?" the Professor asks. "June we didn't find the key or coin in a well, so why would you think the treasure would be in the other one?"

"Because that isn't the marking of a well, it's this!" I say pointing to the interlinking rings on the top of the key.

"I'm almost positive it was a well marking," Dr Cooke shakes his head. "It was a loopy 'W'– we all thought so."

"But what if it *wasn't*. Think about it," I urge them. "The first marking was right on the edge of the paper where it was torn. The top of the marking could have been ripped off. The document was in terrible shape. There were spots all over were the ink had been worn off."

"I don't know, if Josie were the one to know where the treasure was, why wouldn't she have gone and got it?" he argues.

"She never would have been able to spend it," I say to them. "Everyone would have known where the coins came from and she couldn't have moved around like men did in that time to trade them. Maybe she wasn't over Cassidy and her sister running off together and thumbed her nose at him by burying the treasure. Or he left it with her and was planning to return for it when things cooled down. This whole time we assumed that Cassidy buried the treasure, but what if he left it with Josie when he went to South America and she was the one who buried it?"

"She was the one to draw the map," the Professor says, standing up to join me. "That box could have belonged to her."

"We assumed it was Butch's, but perhaps she made it. Her father was a blacksmith," Dr Cooke says joining us.

"It has to be," I say to them.

"It's our last shot," Dr Cooke says, biting his lip. "They'll be here in a few hours and we won't be able to go back on that land."

"We better hope we're right then," the Professor picks up his hat.

Chapter Seventeen

"But, it's pitch dark out!" Clint moans as we saddle the horses. "And it's raining!"

"It's just a light drizzle," I say to him, trying to temper my anger.

Honestly, I've been digging all day and didn't have the luxury of a nap, but you don't see me complaining.

"Can't this wait? It's like three in the morning!" he complains.

Dr Cooke and the Professor both pull themselves onto their mounts and I narrow my eyes at Clint.

"No, Clint. It can't. Because in exactly," I look down at my watch, "Five hours and forty-eight minutes the Antichrist will be walking through that door and your high hopes for being the next YouTube sensation will be in the bin."

I pull myself up onto the horse and the animal seems to sense my urgency. It stomps its feet, ready to move.

"Let's ride!" I yell, putting my heels to the horses flank. The animal leaps forward and I am nearly thrown off the back by the sudden motion.

Not daring to look back, I trust the others are following as we cross the ridge, go down the hill, and enter the forest at a full gallop. The horse seems to know the direction since we've been here so often and goes of his own accord. I hold the compass up to try and see it, but the jostling of the horse below me makes the task useless. I decide to ride on for a bit longer before we will stop and check our coordinates.

The sounds of hooves approach from behind, and I turn to see the Professor pull up beside me.

"Ma'am," he says, tipping the brim of his hat to me.

I raise an eyebrow to Dr Cooke who has also come even with us, we all stop when we arrive at a wide clearing.

"It shouldn't be too far from here," I say, as we pull our horses to a stop. "We've been riding for nearly half an hour, so the stream should only be a few kilometres away now."

"And how far away was the second marking?" Dr Cooke asks.

"I think about half a kilometre, give or take," I say, looking around as the rain falls more heavily on us without the protection of the thick dense trees.

"What exactly are we looking for again?" Clint asks, as he takes his camera out of the saddlebag and starts filming the area.

"We're not *entirely* sure," I respond, looking around me. "But it would probably have a marking in a tree of the interlinking rings."

Clint's eyes widen.

201

"That's *it*?" he asks. "That's *all* you know?"

"Well… yes," I say, shrugging but try to smile like the task isn't as overwhelming as it sounds.

It's not overwhelming, it's impossible.

"There are thousands of trees in this place," he says, and I see he now has the camera trained on my face.

"Yes, I realize that. But it's not like we are searching the whole forest. Just this area," I say, indicating the trees in front of me. "And over there… and maybe over there…"

I look down at the compass in my hand as though it might help me.

"June, was there anything you remember about the map—about some sort of landmark nearby?" Dr Cooke asks.

I close my eyes and envision Josie Bassett's map hanging in the museum as though it were in front of me. "There was a small path that led to it off of a large clearing," I say, opening my eyes. "If she knew the direction to be accurate it should be off to the North here."

I carefully get down off of my horse and take a tentative step towards the dark narrow passage in front of me. We've always stuck more to the trails on the horses. There is no way they would fit down this narrow grouping of trees with the saddlebags.

"Do you think she would have left her horse?" I turn to the Professor.

He frowns from on top of his horse as it moves from side to side below him, growing uneasy from the heavy rain.

"Her cabin was on the other side of this forest. Perhaps it's wider approaching from the South," he suggests.

I nod absently, thinking of our options when a branch in front of us snaps loudly.

The horse pulls at the reins I hold in my hand and snorts, stomping his feet.

"What was that?" Clint says in a tight croak.

"It's just a branch. The rain puts weight on them and they snap," I say, trying to reassure him but ducking at the sound of a large screech as an owl swoops down overhead.

I stand up straight again and turn to the others when a large crack rings in the air and the horses have finally had enough.

The Professor's mount rears his front legs, kicking them furiously out in front of him and I step back trying not to get struck by one of the hooves. The Professor lands in a heap behind the horse and doesn't move as the animal sprints off in the direction we just came from.

Clint struggles to keep a hold of the reins of his horse, but the animal's back legs keep pushing off the ground trying to buck its rider off.

I take a step towards the Professor, but Dr Cooke who managed to get off his horse reaches him first. He puts his hands under the Professor's arms, dragging him over to a nearby tree for protection from the flailing hooves that seem to be coming from every direction.

I look up to see Clint's head is a messy blur, his body

whipped from one direction to the other as small squeals of alarm come from his mouth.

"Hold on!" I yell to Clint, realizing the other three horses are no longer in sight.

This was obviously the wrong thing to say, as just after I yell it, Clint lets go of the reins and his body flails off the horse like a rag doll, landing hard on his rear. The horse, now aware that he's managed to dismount his rider, gives a final whimper and bolts in the direction the other horses went.

"Are you alright?" I ask Clint, who is shaking his head, causing water droplets to sprinkle around him.

"I—I think so," he says, raising his arms to assess the damage. "Camera made it!"

He holds up the recording device, the red light is still blinking.

I turn to look at the Professor, who is hunched over against the tree as Dr Cooke holds a handkerchief up to his forehead.

"He's got a nasty gash," Dr Cooke says, nodding to the handkerchief. "But I don't think anything's broken."

"Professor," I say, shaking his shoulder with no response.

"He's breathing, I think he's just been knocked out," Dr Cooke says and looks up at our surroundings as the rain picks up. "We should get him under better cover."

"I got his hat," Clint says, passing me the Professor's

hat.

"Thanks," I say, taking it from his outstretched hand.

"The horses are gone," he says, matter of fact.

"We'll have to go for help, June," Dr Cooke says looking at me. "We don't know the full extent of his injuries and—"

"I'll stay with him," I nod.

"No, I'll stay with him," Dr Cooke argues. "You're younger and you know the map better."

I shake my head.

"I should be here when he wakes up," I say, looking down at the Professor. "You go for help."

"June…" Dr Cooke puts his hand on my shoulder and I can tell he wants to argue more.

"Please, we don't know what is wrong with him. We can't waste time arguing," I say, patting his hand. "We will be fine. We will stay right here and wait for you to come back."

Dr Cooke studies me, but eventually nods.

"Clint and I will be back as soon as we can," he assures me.

Chapter Eighteen

The rain pelts down around us and I huddle closer to the Professor. At least the tree foliage is protecting us from the worst of it.

A few minutes later I feel the Professor stir beside me, and I lift my head to see his eyes slowly crack open.

"Professor?" I say, sitting up straighter. "How are you feeling?"

"That was some mighty potent scotch, I think," he says, lifting his hand to the side of his head and wincing.

"You fell and hit your head," I say. "Just rest, help is coming for us."

He nods but I can see he doesn't really comprehend what I am saying.

A look of panic comes across his features and he reaches into the breast pocket of his jacket. I see him visibly relax as he brings out his leather bound journal and a pen.

"I've really cocked up, this time, huh?" I say, leaning my head against the tree behind me.

"Mmm," the Professor nods noncommittally as he writes in his journal.

"The coins could be anywhere..." I say, gesturing

around the dark forest before us.

The Professor continues to scratch his pen.

"Even if Dr Cooke and Clint find help, it could be hours before they're back—maybe not until morning," I say, pulling my knapsack onto my knee. "With my luck, bloody Phillip will find us here and have us personally escorted off the property."

"Who?" he looks up, frowning.

"Phillip, the man who's trying to ruin my career," I say, and when I can see there is no recognition on his face I add, "The one with the nice hair."

The Professor nods, but I can tell he doesn't know who I am talking about.

"I just thought, if I could find those coins… if I could show Oxford and the world that I am just as capable as him—"

The Professor flips a page of his journal, and smiles. He picks up a small photograph and holds it out to me.

It's a picture of me on Christmas day when I was nine. The edges are thin, and there is a small rip in the top corner. He's obviously held it many times. I'm looking down in wonderment at the present in front of me. I remember it so well. The Professor had just returned home from a site in Egypt. He wasn't supposed to make it home in time for Christmas morning, but he had arrived late the night before to surprise me.

He brought me home my first tool set. It contained a

small chisel, hammer, magnifying glass and a variety of small brushes all wrapped up in a soft brown leather pouch. I still have it at home tucked up on top of a box in the closet. I thought maybe I would give it to my child some day.

"That's my granddaughter. My June Bug," he says, smiling at the picture. "Isn't she lovely?"

I feel the tears at the back of my eyes and nod, looking at the picture.

"I gave her that last Christmas, she wants to be an archaeologist," he says, gently rubbing his thumb over my face in the picture.

"Like her grandfather," I smile at him.

"Hmm," he nods.

"Would you—Would you like that?" I say, tilting my head to the side to better study his features.

His brow creases a little, but the smile remains.

"I want her to be whatever will make her happy," he shrugs. "But I won't say I'm sorry that it seems to be history."

My smile widens and he laughs.

"She's a good girl, my June Bug. I'm not able to be there a lot for her," he says with regret. "She goes to an all girls school for much of the year, and I know she doesn't like it. I wish I could be there more, but the archaeological community is at such a critical stage, with new technology and gadgets it's not far off that what I do will be obsolete. I need to contribute all that I can now, so that the world will see how important our field of study is, so that it's still here for her future."

"I'm sure you're there when it matters," I say, putting my hand on his arm.

"She tries to take on the world; show me how responsible she can be so I will take her with me when I leave," the smile slowly fades from his face and I can see tears form in his eyes. "I don't want to leave her, but I have to."

The tears escape from my lashes as I look at the beautiful man in front of me, the man that did the best that he could to raise me. And now, as I sit here and reminisce with him about a little girl we both knew so long ago, I know that he is going to be leaving me again soon for entirely different reasons.

"I think she understands," I say, using my other hand to hold his tight.

"She'll be fine, of course," he says, smiling at me. "She's used to being on her own. She's a survivor—I always say there's nothing my little June Bug can't manage once she's put her mind to it. But she never knew her mother or father, and I just don't like the thought of no one being there for her. No matter how strong we are, there are times that we all need someone to lean on."

I pat his hand, not knowing what to say.

"And God bless anyone who tries to help her!" he chuckles again. "Last summer I took her with me to the University while I was teaching a summer lecture. She was getting a little bored in the lessons—she has an eidetic memory, you know; it's the most remarkable thing. Well, she has already made her way through most of the books in my library, she's a very bright pupil. I watched the students struggle with concepts that June has had mastered for at least a year. So instead of her sitting in lecture listening to things she already knew I created a treasure map for her."

I sit up a little straighter on the hard, cold ground. I had forgotten about the treasure hunt.

"I made her a map with clues that brought her all over Oxford. Oh, she loved it," he smiles at me with such satisfaction. "She completed half of it the first day, but then got stuck on one of the clues in the library. She didn't sleep that whole night."

"I remember," I nod, but the Professor seems not to hear me.

"She scoured all the books in the library for the answer. Drove the librarian mad trying to keep up with putting them all away," he laughs. "Some of the students would try to help her, but she wouldn't hear of it. It took her three weeks to figure out where to find the next clue, and do you know where the answer was? It wasn't in a book, it was hanging on the wall right behind the librarian."

I close my eyes slowly. I remember the feeling of both exhilaration and utter disappointment in myself when I finally saw the sign hanging up behind Mrs Fowl's desk. I remember cursing under my breath; living alone with an adult male my entire life, I had picked up quite a few choice words at the tender age of nine. The librarian had clucked at me with each new book I pulled off a shelf. I thought she obviously didn't understand the importance of my task, but really it must have been because she knew the clue wasn't in any of the books—the Professor had asked her to hang the poster—and I was creating a lot of unwarranted work for her. She had asked me several times a day if I needed help looking for something, and I'd emphatically told her no. I'd thought I would never find the next clue and it had been right in front of me all along: if I'd only just looked up.

"She'll have to find a head strong lad to keep her on her toes," he says, slipping the photo back into his journal.

"She seems to like her independence. Maybe she's meant to be alone," I say to him, sitting back to rest my head on the tree again and trying to banish the image of Griffin from my mind.

"Oh, no. Of course, some people don't mind it—I've been a bachelor since my Josephine went nearly five years ago now," he says closing his journal and putting it on his lap. "But I wouldn't wish that on June. She deserves to have someone realize she's the moon and the stars."

My eyes look up to the dark, black sky and search for some source of light.

I've buggered up a lot of things in my life, but sitting here with the Professor, there is only one thing that seems to be a real regret. Griffin deserved so much more than I gave him, and I hope that someday soon I will be able to tell him that.

"I've tried my best with her. I got it right sometimes, I think; but sometimes I have not," he looks down at his journal and places his palm flat against the cover. "That's why I write in this, about my life, about her. Because whether or not you get it right or wrong, what's most important is that you tried with all that you had. And I hope in the end, she knows I tried so desperately for her."

I look past the glass spectacles into the earnest clear blue eyes. He has done remarkable things, seen marvellous wonders, and in the midst of that, unbeknownst to me, really only ever had one true focus.

"She knows," I say, placing my hand once again on top of his.

***

I jerk awake at the sound of a snapping branch.

"Nothing, June Bug," the Professor pats my head. "Seems like some sort of large possum."

"Oh," I say, sitting up straighter. I'm not sure I feel any more reassured now knowing what the animal is. "Have I been asleep long?"

I rub my eyes and look around, but the night is still pitch black.

"Oh, I don't think so," he shrugs, twirling a long piece of grass around his finger.

"How's your head?" I say, looking up at the gash. "It's not bleeding anymore."

"It's fine," he says, waving away my concern. "I rather think we should get up and try and make our way back if you're done resting."

I shake my head, but the Professor is already starting to rise.

"I don't think that is a good idea," I say, also making my way to my feet. "The first rule when you're lost is to stay in the same spot. If we move, how will Dr Cooke find us again?"

"June, if we wait for Daniel to bring help we'll die here from old age!" he says, clicking his tongue reproachfully. "No, the best course of action is pro-action."

"I'm not sure if that is actually a word," I say, following behind him.

"It is," he says, waving away my argument. "Now, which way would you say is East?"

We both look up at the dark sky, searching for any constellations that may give us a hint to our location.

"There's not one light in the sky!" I say in frustration and spin around, trying to get a view from all directions.

I see a small glint of light off to the right. I shake my head and try and pick out what it was that caught my attention. Searching the dark tree trunks to no avail, I decide I must have imagined it. But there, just out of the corner of my eye, I see it again, and I squint at the large gap in the trees in the distance.

"Professor," I say, pulling his arm to get his attention.

"Do you see—"

He follows my outstretched finger, frowning.

I squint my eyes, and gasp as a thin beam of light glints off the small metal piece fifty feet away. I walk the clearing, the Professor close behind me.

"June, what is—"

I stop dead, not believing my eyes.

There, thirty feet in front of me, is a stone with the small metal marking embedded in it.

"It's the marking. The same one that's on the box, that's on the key," I say, turning to look at the Professor in disbelief. "We've found it!"

Not waiting for him to comment, I dash forward to the marker, afraid it will disappear if I take my eyes off of it for even a moment.

"June, wait!" the Professor says, and I turn to look back at his face—but the world falls out from underneath me.

Chapter Nineteen

I land with a thud and groan from the sharp pain in my left leg. I look down, but can't see anything besides murky, black liquid that sits just below my waist. It looks so thick, almost like oil, but as I run my hand through it I feel it has the consistency of water. I tentatively feel for my left leg. My thigh seems alright, but as my hand travels past my knee I feel the odd angle that my calf is sitting at and I have to control the gag that comes from my throat.

"June, are you alright?" the Professor's head materializes in the small hole that outlines the night sky. "June, answer me!"

"I—," I clear my throat as my words come out in a croak. "I'm fine. I think... I think I've broken my leg."

"Christ almighty," the Professor's head shakes, and my vision blurs. "I thought you were dead."

I look at the mud caked wall surrounding me, spanning not more than two feet on either side of me. Running my hands up the walls I feel something a foot above my head that feels like old, rotten lumber. Careful to keep the weight on my right leg, I again put my hands below the water line at my waist and feel around, but I can only feel the slick walls of dirt.

"I think it's a well," I say, trying to project my voice up to him. "I guess it really was just a marking for the water supply on the map."

The laugh gets stuck in my throat and I lean on the wall to try and take further pressure off of my broken bone.

"Never mind that, how the bloody hell are we going to get you out?" the Professor's voice booms down.

"I don't know," I say, running my fingers down the wet lumber only to have a layer crumble away in my hand. "I don't think I'll be able to climb out."

"I should think not. That must be a fifteen foot drop."

I nod, thinking his guess to be accurate. I look down and realize that the waist deep water I landed in probably saved me even further broken bones, possibly even my life.

"There are support beams, but they've rotted away…" I yell up to him.

"What are we—" I hear the panic in his voice and his head disappears from the opening.

"Professor!" I yell.

His head doesn't appear and a sense of panic mixed with claustrophobia starts to consume me.

"Professor!" I yell again, trying to push the wet walls further away from me.

His head suddenly appears again and my body relaxes slightly.

"Don't you worry, little lady, I'll get you out of there in two shakes," he says, tipping his hat to me with a thick American accent.

"Uhh…" I frown.

"Just getting my rope ready to lasso down to you," he says. "Then I'll pull you up."

"What rope?" I frown and start to feel like the distance to the top feels much further.

"A cowboy always keeps a rope tied to his horse," he explains.

"The horses are gone!" I yell up to him.

His head lifts and he looks around. "So they are," he concedes.

"Look, Mr Wayne—" I say.

"Please, call me John," he smiles back to me.

I sigh and wipe a mud caked hand across my forehead. "Can you maybe find a really long branch… or maybe a vine," I suggest hopefully, even though I know how pointless the request is.

"I could try…" he says, and his head disappears again.

I search around in a futile effort, looking for anything that might not crumble under my fingertips.

I jump as a loud crash sounds from above.

"What was that?" I yell up.

I wince as the mud from my forehead runs into my eyes.

"What's that?" His head appears again, as more splatters of water falls down on me.

"Did a tree fall?" I ask. "I heard a loud crashing noise."

"Oh no, that was thunder," he looks up to the sky, and I have to squint to see his face through the pellets of rain coming down. "I think a storm is coming."

"Oh my God," I say, the panic finally coming to the surface. I frantically run my hands down the mud wall. "Get me out! Get me out!"

I scream over and over again, and the more I run my hands over the wall, the more comes down in wet glops beside me.

"I'll go for help," the Professor yells down to me, a sense of urgency completely missing from his voice.

"No, please!" I scream up to him. "Please don't leave me!"

His face doesn't reappear, and I begin to sob as the water rises, inch by inch.

There's one good thing about the water rising, I realize: weight is taken off of my broken leg. Maybe I could tread water enough to stay afloat until the Professor comes back. If he ever comes back.

No, I refuse to believe that. No matter what is happening, no matter who he thinks he is, on some level he knows me. He wouldn't leave me. Not like this.

The rain is coming down so hard now it's difficult to look up. The water has risen past my chest and my arms have started to push the water away from around me out of pure instinct. I tentatively move my left leg and cry out in pain. I might have been able to tread water with two good legs, but not with a broken one. I look around again at the dark brown walls, not sure if it is the rain or my tears that are blinding my vision.

I look down at the black water below me, willing it to lighten and reveal some sort of refuge, some foot hole to give me hope.

A foot hole. That's it. If I can find a foot hole maybe I could hoist myself up slightly and try and find something higher to grab onto. It's a long shot, but at this point it's my only shot.

I make my decision and take slow deep breaths. I'll have to feel around with my hands. The option of standing on my left leg is impossible and I don't think I could use it to feel around below the water.

Taking one final deep breath, I push my face below the surface and close my eyes.

My hands reach for the wall as I try and feel around for any nook that I could rest my foot in. My left leg sends shooting pains up my back but I force myself not to focus on it and concentrate instead on my fingers. I feel to the left, slowly turning myself around as I rub up and down the wall. I think I feel a piece of rock but when I rub my hand over it, more of the wall crumbles.

I bring my head up, breaking the surface and taking a long deep breath of the muggy air as the rain barrels down on top of me. The water reaches my chin now, and I tip back my head, trying to escape the suffocating feeling of the water all around my body. I'm forced to tread water and every jostle of my left leg causes me to cry out in pain.

I stifle back another sob and admit that I can't do this. I'm going to drown in this hole.

I'm not going to see Griffin again. I'm not going to be able to tell him how sorry I am, how I messed everything up and it was my fault—all of it. He won't know how much I love him, and given the chance to do it again, I would show him he is my stars and my moon.

I'm not going to see the Professor again. He won't have anyone to look after him, to tell him to the very last day how loved he is. That he did well. More than well, and he can rest now with no regrets.

The tears pour down the sides of my face as the pain and sadness clog my throat and causes me to splutter the rising water levels.

Looking up at the dark night sky, hazed by the ceaseless waterfall, I take one last deep breath and submerge my head.

I let myself relax, taking all the weight off of my limbs as my body falls into a sitting position and I sink to the bottom. My bum hits the floor and I will my eyes to remain closed and try and relax as best as I can.

My hands reach for the ground beside me to steady my body. My left palm encounters something that feels rough and I turn my head and open my eyes. I can't see anything through the dark murky water, but my right hand instinctively reaches for the same spot as the left. My finger tips feel around and they come across a smooth wood surface. Quickly, and seemingly of their own accord, my hands trace the outside of the small wooden crate, until they find the metal handles. With what seems my last bit of energy I pull the box onto my lap.

Without seeing it, I know what I hold in my hands. I've found my treasure, and it's cost me everything.

Large clumps of what I can only assume are mud fall down through the water around me, putting a further weight on my body. I register that the weight of the water is causing enough pressure that the well's walls are collapsing.

My body convulses and without my mind's consent, my body tries to push itself to the surface, willing the air the enter its lungs.

I feel one last convulsion and then the world around me gets darker. Much darker than I have ever known. And then… nothing.

Chapter Twenty

My body feels weightless as I drift higher and higher into the unknown until I drop quite suddenly. I feel as though I break a barrier and then everything seems crisp and brighter. I try and open my eyes, to look up into the brightness that is taking me home, but they seem glued shut and I have neither the energy nor the will to open them.

I hear something in the distance and I try and force my ears to work. The noise gets louder as a large weight pushes on my chest. Suddenly a warm muggy gust of air is forced down my throat and I desperately want to cough.

"June!" I hear the noise more clearly now, it seems so close and it is screaming my name.

I tilt my head back and am finally able to cough, choking on a mixture of water and air.

I turn my head to the side as my lungs burn with the effort of trying to get oxygen through the coughing fit.

I feel a rough hand push the hair off the side of my face and my eyes open slowly to see the image of Griffin's face.

"I was hoping you would be my heaven," I slur my words, a smile curving the side of my lips.

"Are you alright?" he asks, and his blurry face frowns

with worry.

"Am I—" I try and blink to form the words. "Am I dead?"

"What? No," he runs his hands over my face over and over again. "Christ June, you nearly drowned."

"I, I fell into a well," I frown and try to sit up but my body feels likes rubber.

"I know, I found the Professor wandering around over there," he points to the distance. "Or it was over there… oh who the hells knows where we are. Didn't know his ass from his elbow, or where you were. I started wandering and calling your name, and then I saw his hat at the opening of that well. I didn't… Christ."

I blink, trying to comprehend his words.

So, I'm not dead. I'm alive. Or this is my mind's idea of a very cruel joke.

"God, June, if I had found you a minute later—" he breaks off in a sob, and holds me in his arms so tightly I am not sure if I can breathe again.

My body begins to rack with my own sobs as I realize how true his words were.

"I'm so sorry," he puts his cheek next to mine and its warmth feels so good against my skin. "I came back and Pearl said you were gone and the horses were missing. I took the only horse left in the stable to come and find you."

"I'm sorry," I say, trying to shake my head. "It's all my fault. I never should have—"

"Shh," he says, stroking my hair over and over again to reassure both of us that I am alive and well. "It's going to be alright now."

"No, it's not alright. Everything you said was true. My career, the treasure, nothing is more important than you," I argue.

I jolt and pull back slightly to look down at my hands.

"The treasure," I whisper, and frown trying to remember.

Did I imagine it? Did I hallucinate, thinking it was the last moments of my life, trying to give myself some form of comfort?

"What? What's wrong?" he says, looking at the ground around me.

"I found it," I say hesitantly, and then my voice gets more steady the more sure I am that it was real. "It was at the bottom of the well. I found the box."

I can almost feel the heavy weight in my hands again.

"In the well?" Griffin frowns and turns his head to look down at the ground where the opening is.

"Yes, but—wait!" I yell as Griffin disentangles himself from me and quickly walks over to a long rope that is tied to large tree with the marker embedded in it. "What are you doing?"

He walks over to the hole and looks down before dropping the long rope into it.

"You can't go in there!" I yell at him, and try and will my

arms to push my body up right.

"June, they will be here any minute, and that well's walls are collapsing. If I don't get that box now, you won't ever get it. They'll come here, and dig it up themselves and this will all be for naught!" he says, and I can almost feel him willing me to agree.

"I don't care!" I yell, and realize that I truly mean it. "It's not worth losing you for some stupid treasure. You are worth so much more than that!"

He looks at me and smiles before turning around and disappearing into the hole.

"No!" I scream, and jerk my body in the direction of the hole. The rain is still pouring and the ground is so wet that my hand slips out from beneath me. I scream again from the searing pain in my leg, but I don't stop. Inch my inch I pull my body over the soaking earth.

"Griffin! Griffin!" I yell over and over, but the rope down the well remains motionless.

I'm still at least ten feet away when I hear a rustling through the forest. I turn and my arms almost melt with relief.

"Professor!" I yell, and his head whips up at the sound of his name.

"June, there you are! I must have taken a wrong turn," he says, looking around with a confused expression. "Why are you on the ground?"

"I've broken my leg," I say, weakly pointing to it.

"Griffin has gone back in the well, you have to pull him up!"

"The well?" he looks at my leg, perplexed. "What have you two gotten up to?"

"Professor, please!" I yell at him, as he comes closer. "The well, there, Griffin's in it and you have to pull him up."

The Professor walks over to the well and peers inside.

"Don't see anything," he says, looking back at me and shaking his head. "Are you sure?"

"Yes, I'm sure!" I try and continue to drag my body over toward the opening.

The Professor peers over again and jumps back as a large part of the ground beneath his foot gives way and tumbles into the opening.

"Careful, it's starting to collapse," I say sharply. "Is he there? Do you see him?"

"No I don't see– oh wait, there he is," the Professor stretches his neck over the opening. "Griffin my lad, how goes it?"

I can't make out the reply but I hear the low garbled noise.

"Right, jolly good," the Professor nods and turns to me. "He's coming up."

I look and see the rope tighten and slowly wiggle back and forth as more earth crumbles around it. I hold my breath until I see his fingertips grasp the ground around the opening.

His mud caked face emerges and he hoists himself over

the clearing. My body sags in relief.

"You bloody idiot!" I yell, tears streaming down my face. "You could have died!"

Griffin ignores this, instead choosing to address the Professor.

"The walls are crumbling. I had to climb out and pull June up with the rope tied around her middle and it's disturbed the integrity of the walls. We need to get it out now or it will be buried. We'd never have enough time to dig it out before Phillip gets here in the morning."

"Right, I was tug-o-war champ in the sixth form," the Professor says, rolling up his sleeves.

"I can help!" I say, trying to lift my torso off the ground.

"You stay back," Griffin orders, and takes the rope. "I tied it around the box, but it weighs a bloody ton!"

The Professor just nods and picks up the rope from behind Griffin.

"Right, heave!" Griffin yells and projects a loud noise as his arms strain to pull the rope. "Again!"

I watch as the two men pull the rope, gaining a foot or so with each pull.

They pull, and they pull, and they pull. My mind wants to get up and help, but the pain in my body and my heavy wet clothes makes me stay put.

"It's nearly there! Just a few more tugs," Griffin says through gritted teeth.

Then my breath catches in my throat as the muddy

ground slips out from beneath his foot, causing him to fall on his back and let go of the rope.

"Griffin, are you alright?"

The Professor's arms shake with the effort to hold onto the rope, but the look of concentration on his face is so focused. He places one hand over the next and pulls the rope to his chest. He lets out a final loud groan and the box slips over the ridge to sit perfectly still on the dark, brown earth.

"We did it," I say, as Griffin gets up, and tentatively makes his way over to the box, pulling it further from the opening. "We found the treasure."

"Well technically we found a box," the Professor points out. "Shall we just confirm what's inside?"

I look up into his smiling face as a shrill voice rings through the trees.

"Albert! June!" Dr Cooke's voice booms to our left. "Where the bloody hell are they?"

We hear another mumbled voice, which I assume is Clint.

"No, we left them just around here. I have the internal compass of Christopher Columbus," Dr Cooke snaps as he emerges through the trees with Clint, each of them leading a horse.

"Daniel!" the Professor waves, flapping his hands back and forth even though they've already seen us.

"There you are!" Dr Cooke says in relief. "We've been looking everywhere for you! You won't believe what we've bloody been through!"

"I can only imagine," I say, and despite myself I laugh in relief.

"Clint nearly got us bloody killed—led us down a path that ended in a fifty foot drop… Could have died," he scowls at the young intern who looks too exhausted to care about the tongue lashing.

"Never mind that now," the Professor waves his story away as Dr Cooke comes to stand beside us. "We've found it, Daniel. We found the treasure!"

Dr Cooke's eyes widen in astonishment before they finally make contact with the wooden crate in front of us.

He drops to his knees, his eyes never leaving the small golden marking embedded in the top.

"Look at the dovetail joints. The wood is in remarkable condition. Is it—is it the coins?" he whispers, finally bringing his eyes to meet mine.

"It has the marking," I say to him before looking at the Professor. "But there is really only one way to find out."

"Chester, get me the key," the Professor says with a wide smile.

Clint quickly goes to the side of his bag that's strapped to one of the horses he managed to find and comes back with the gold key and the video camera, trying to capture each of our faces.

"Go on then," I say to the Professor, urging him on.

He looks down at the key in his hand and shakes his

head.

"No, you do it," he says dropping it in my palm.

I look up at Griffin who's smile is immense.

"Do you want—" I start to ask him, holding out the key.

"Oh would someone just open the bloody thing!" Clint yells and causes me to jump and nearly drop the key.

Griffin laughs and turns the chest so the keyhole is facing me.

I smile at him, my chin wobbling, before I insert the key and turn.

There is a quick clink from the lock unlatching, and I push on the lid, forcing it up.

"Good God," I say, as I take in piles of gold coins spilling out of a worn, threadbare bag inside the chest. "The lost treasure of Butch Cassidy."

"We found it," Dr Cooke says, wrapping his arm around the Professor's shoulders. "We did it, June."

"We did," I say, smiling at Griffin through tear blurred eyes.

Chapter Twenty-One

My shoulders slump in relief as we cross over the last ridge and Pearl's house comes into sight. I nearly passed out multiple times on the journey back, my head lolling from side to side with every movement of the horse. Griffin found a long, thick branch and managed to tie my broken leg to it with the rope to try and stop it from moving, but anytime my eye catches the sight of the odd angle my head swims, and I feel I might throw up. Griffin's arm is wrapped tightly around my waist as I lean back on his chest. He's actually a very good rider which has brought me a little comfort on the journey.

A dark mass seems to be looming in front of Pearl's house and after a few more moments my vision clears and I see it is a group of people, with Phillip, looking smug, front and centre.

Well, he actually looks a bit concerned, but I know underneath that mask he is loving every minute of this. Bastard.

"Wonderful," I mutter under my breath as the horses make their way over to the house.

Stopping twenty feet from the group, Griffin swings

himself down from the horse before turning around to wrap his arms around me.

I gingerly transfer my weight from the horse to his waiting arms and my broken leg swings slightly from the weight of the branch.

I cry out in pain and feel my stomach rise up to my throat.

"June, you're hurt!" Pearl yells in alarm and quickly rushes up to us.

"I'm fine," I try and assure her, but she grabs hold of my free hand.

"I'm so glad I sent your man out for you," she says. "I came home to find him banging on the door, the horses gone, and not even a note!"

"I'm so sorry I worried you," I say, squeezing her hand. "But, I am glad you sent him out after me."

I turn my smiling face to Griffin and kiss him, trying to thank him over and over again with the gesture.

He returns the smile as I pull back my face and jostles me a little as he tries to regain his grip on my body.

"And just look at you all—why you ain't fit to sleep with the pigs looking like that!"

I laugh and look down. She's right. Between our wet, mud soaked clothes, my matted hair and the blood still staining the side of the Professor's face I would say we probably look a right sight coming over the ridge on the horses.

"Did you find it, June?" she lowers her voice, but the note of anticipation still rings through. "Did you find the treasure?"

My face splits into the widest grin yet.

"We found it," I say, pointing behind me. We fashioned a small sled-like creation with a few well chosen logs and the left over rope to put the treasure on to pull. Clint rode behind, filming the laughter and conversation from the riders the whole way back.

"Yippee!" she exclaims, jumping in the air from exhilaration. "I knew you would, I knew you would find it!"

I look to Griffin, who beams at me. The Professor and Dr Cooke once again congratulate each other with handshakes and slaps on the back.

"I don't believe it!" I look and see Phillip, looking like someone let all of the air out of him. "There's no way you found it– I don't believe it!"

"Well believe it, you pompous arse!" the Professor says and walks over to open the lid of the box, running his fingers through the coins.

"But... but... *how?*" the frown on Phillip's face reveals how incomprehensible the notion is to him that someone other than himself would be able to find such treasure.

"We used something we rely on very heavily in our family," I say. "Our brains."

He narrows his eyes as me, but his gaze quickly returns to the coins.

"June! What is going on here?" The crowd parts and my eyes widen.

"Professor Dockery," I say, not quite believing the Dean of Oxford University is standing in front of me in the foothills of Colorado. "What are you doing here?"

"What am *I* doing here?" he says shaking his head. "What in the blazes are *you* doing here?"

"I—"

"I've been told some wild stories over the past few weeks, stories I didn't believe until this very minute!" His wrinkled face looks completely overwhelmed. "Did you really coerce the information out of my assistant and steal this assignment from Phillip?"

"I—I would hardly say *coerce*," I say, thinking back to my conversation with Julia. It feels like a lifetime ago.

"June, this is not how a Professor at Oxford conducts themselves!" he says, each angry word spat from his lips.

"I'm sorry, it's only—"

"It wasn't her," Dr Cooke says, coming to stand beside me. "Dr Albert Jenson and I take complete and full responsibility."

"Absolutely," the Professor nods, taking his handkerchief out of his pocket and wiping his brow before turning to Dr Cooke. "Responsibility for what?"

Dr Cooke mumbles under his breath and raises his eyes to the heavens.

"No, they are lying," I say, trying to force my torso to sit up straighter in Griffin's arms. "This whole thing was my idea. They knew nothing of it and I take full responsibility for the consequences."

Dr Dockery looks from the two men back to me.

"You are fired," he says.

I recoil in shock. Fired? I've never been fired from anything before in my life.

"You can't fire her!" Griffin says into the silence. "She found the treasure!"

"I don't care," he says, shaking his head. "What you did was wrong and I cannot condone it, no matter what the excuse or result was."

"But—" Griffin starts.

"No, you're right," I say, placing my hand on Griffin's chest and turning to Dr Dockery. "What I did was wrong."

"June," Griffin starts to argue.

"No, this is what is right," I say, nodding to him.

Dr Dockery turns and walks away.

"But what you did was wrong as well," I yell after him and he stops in his tracks to turn back to me.

"Excuse me?"

"I am a renowned historian who has proved over and over again that I am capable of great things. But you let your stuffy old reputation and the press manipulate you into making the wrong choices," I argue. "My grandfather spent his life on historical sites so that what we love wouldn't become irrelevant. And now it's happened anyway. You let

235

Phillip here go to all sorts of sites with his fancy cameras and television crew because of the great press it brings to the University. But that isn't what archaeology is about."

"My fans don't seem to complain," Phillip says to the woman standing next to me, flashing her a bright white smile.

"Your prejudice against me and my family for the bad press we caused you—which by the way, wasn't even our bloody fault to begin with—hasn't just cost me my career. Think how much history is out there, waiting to be discovered. I was only asking for a chance to help you discover it."

"And this was the right method to get across that message?" he says, his arms crossed in front of him. "Oxford is a University of integrity and decorum. You, as a Professor, should know that."

"No, what I did wasn't right," I say, shaking my head. "But what you did wasn't right either."

Dr Dockery sniffs once, before turning around and making his way back through the crowd.

I take a deep breath and turn to see Phillip staring at me.

"You know June, I have a lot of resources outside of the University," he shrugs. "I know your heart was in the right place, and I personally feel somewhat responsible for this little mix up."

I clear my throat to avoid saying anything.

"It won't be easy—I'll have to call in a few favours of course," he shakes head back as the breeze plays with his wavy hair. "But I'm going to make it my personal mission to find you another position at a different University."

He looks around the group, seemingly waiting for a round of applause.

"And why would you do that?" I ask, raising my eyebrow.

"June, honestly," he says, putting his hand to his heart. "You wound me. I thought we were friends, and that's just something friends do for each other."

I hear Pearl snort beside me.

"And what do you want from June here?" Pearl asks, her hands on her hip.

"Nothing," he says emphatically. "Just knowing you are settled and happy is more thanks than I will ever require."

I narrow my eyes at him.

"That's very generous of you," I say without a note of appreciation in my voice.

"I can imagine you will be quite busy with your dissertation about this discovery," he says, looking over to the wooden crate with the coins inside. "And with your leg injured. I hope you aren't taking too much on."

"I'll manage," I say.

"You know," he put his finger up as though a thought has just occurred to him. "I've done countless hours of research on this subject. Perhaps I could help you with your paper. Maybe a little foreword from me would help you gain some readership on it."

My nostrils flare and I'm not sure whether it's entirely from his words or the fact my leg just jerked in anger.

"That's it! I'm going to kick your ass– broken leg or not!" I say, and try and worm out of Griffin's arms.

"June, you're going to hurt yourself!" Griffin yells, trying to keep his grip on me.

The loud bang that explodes beside my head causes me to freeze. I blink a few times as the ringing in my ears gets louder.

I can hear the crowd in front of me screaming as they push against each other to get away.

"We settle this with a bullet!" The Professor says, the smoke billowing out from the pistol in his hand, pointed at the sky.

"He's crazy!" I hear Phillip yell as he tries to push past the woman he was smiling at moments ago. "He's trying to shoot me!"

"Well, that can't be good," Dr Cooke says, and carefully takes the gun out of the Professor's hand.

Chapter Twenty-Two

I sigh in mock exasperation and put Griffin's screenplay on my lap as the door to the bedroom opens.

"I'm never going to finish if you keep asking me about it," I say.

My laugh fades as Pearl's head pops through the opening.

"Oh, hi Pearl. Sorry, thought you were Griffin," I push myself up in the bed into a better sitting position.

"Just saw the doctor left," she says and nods at my leg.

"I'll have the cast on for six weeks," I say, rapping my knuckles against the hard white shell that binds my leg. "Still, could be worse."

"And you've booked your flight for tomorrow?" she asks.

"Yes, I feel you must have had enough of us by now," I offer her a smile. "It's been lovely being here though."

My head turns at the sound of a truck backing up outside, its sharp beep warning everyone to steer clear.

"Have they bought more equipment?" I ask her.

"That damn historical society is going to ruin my gardens," Pearl mutters under her breath.

"They want to dig up the well," I tell her, even though they must have told her this already.

"Yeah, and it seems every other damn surface of this property."

I offer her a smile and rub a hand up my arm to try and ward off a sudden chill.

"Do you think there is anything out there besides the coins to find?" I ask.

"Nah, you've found all that's to be had," she says, making her way over to the bed. "Them digging up dirt just makes them look like bigger fools than they already do."

"Is Phillip with them?" I ask, running my finger along the edge of the quilt.

"He's the idiot leading the pack," she mutters, shaking her head. "And he's still wearing that stupid bandage on his head. Says he caught some sort of ricochet from the bullet."

I nod but don't say anything, and she sits down on the edge of the bed.

"You found the treasure, June," she says, patting my hand. "Once you write that paper of yours everyone will know it, too."

"I'm not quite sure I can write that paper," I say, not meeting her eyes. "The Historical Society is a bit angry about the whole gun shooting incident, Phillip's making a production about it, and well… I can't really broadcast how I came to be here in the first place."

"Hmm," Pearl nods.

"They took the coins, then?" I ask her, lifting my gaze.

"Last night," she confirms. "They originally belonged to the State, but they said I would get a finder's fee—like you told me."

"And you're alright with that?" I ask.

"Oh, I've known from the beginning my rights. Those folks from the historical society told me straight off I wouldn't get to keep them."

"But," I frown in confusion. "You know you could fight them, it's not set in stone."

"Well, we came to a little compromise," she smiles. "I gave them the rights to the coins without a fuss and they said they wouldn't press charges against your granddaddy."

"Pearl," I say my eyes widening. "I... I don't know what to say."

"I never intended to do it for the money," Pearl says, sitting back a bit on the foot of the bed. "I did it for principle."

"Principle?"

She leans forward and hands me the box in her hands. My eyes widen and a wide toothy grin spreads across her face.

"Where did you get this?" I whisper. My fingers run over the three small gold interlinking rings set into the top of the lid of a much smaller wooden box then the one I found a few days ago.

"Why, from my late husband's great aunt Josie," she says, clapping her hands.

"His great aunt…" I shake my head. "But… You're related to Josie Bassett?"

"Shoot, we were good pals, me and old Josie," Pearl nods at me. "I met her only four days after me and Tom were married. She met us on her front porch with a wad of tobacco in her cheek and a Winchester in her hands."

A laugh escapes my throat at the thought.

"Josie and I became fast friends, seeing as we were the closest relatives she had around these parts. We lived just in the next town from her back then. The stories she would tell me…" Pearl chuckles. "She was quite an old coot. Half of it was bullshit to be sure, but then she would slip in the truth every now and then which made you think just how much of it could really be true."

"And she gave you this?" I ask, running my fingers over the box again.

"Sure did," she opens the lid to reveal a pile of black and white photograph inside. "Made it herself; she loved to make these boxes all different sizes. That's her."

Pearl hands me a photograph of an elderly lady sitting on a rocker, not looking at the camera. Her white hair is piled loosely up and the front pieces have escaped round her face, much like Pearl wears her hair now.

"This is her sister, Ann," she says, handing me another photo.

I look down at the picture of a young women sitting straight, staring into the lens.

"She was a looker. Of course, Josie was a sweetheart back in her day, but Ann..." Pearl whistles through her teeth. "Ann was a knockout."

I nod and hold onto the edge of the photograph, not knowing what else to say or do.

"Of course you know Josie had relations with Mr Butch, but she knew from the beginning he wasn't the marrying kind, and Josie had always wanted a family. So the two of them parted ways and that was that," Pearl explains. "But then he took up with Miss Ann again and Josie thought it might be a little too close to home, if you know what I mean."

"What happened?" I ask.

"Well, Butch weren't a boy scout, that's for darn sure. But then he went and robbed that damn train and brought a whole heap of trouble down on all of them, you see," Pearl says, taking the picture from my hand. "As Josie told it, Butch came looking for her and asked her to keep the coins safe, to bury them somewhere until he could come back for them."

I knew it! I want to scream, but don't dare break her concentration.

"Then he went off to Argentina with Mr Longabaugh and Ann," Pearl says.

"I thought they went with Etta Price," I say, leaning towards her.

"Don't you believe everything you read in those books

girl," Pearl says, shaking her head. "You take a look at Miss Etta Price and then take a good long stare at Miss Ann and you'll come to realize you're staring at one and the same."

"What happened?" I ask.

"Well, Josie buried them coins like Mr Butch told her to, but when he came back to Utah a few years later having jilted Miss Ann. Josie didn't take too kindly to it," Pearl says, rubbing the side of her nose.

"He came back?" My eyes are so wide at this point I'm surprised they are staying in their sockets.

"Oh he came back alright. Lived here till the day he died. Visited Josie every now and then in the beginning," she says, nodding. "But then Josie wouldn't tell him where she buried them coins and Mr Butch didn't take too kindly to it."

"Why wouldn't she tell him?" I ask.

"Well Josie weren't too happy with Butch taking up with Miss Ann after things ended between Josie and him, but Ann was still family, which made Butch family," Pearl explains. "But when Miss Ann finally made it home after she married someone else claiming Butch abandoned her there, I think Josie finally determined it was time Butch Cassidy finally got what was coming to him."

"So, she never told him where she buried the coins?" I ask.

"Not even on the day he died," Pearl nods. "She never told a soul, kept the little secret to herself and gave herself a good chuckle every now and then with the knowledge."

"What did Butch do when she wouldn't tell him?"

"What could he do?" she shrugs. "He couldn't very well go to the authorities, he was thought to be dead and was better off staying that way. No sense in killing Josie, she was the only one who knew where the coins were."

"And how do you play into this, Pearl?" I ask her. "Did you really find that coin under the tree?"

"I sure did," she smiles, but then the smile fades as sadness comes into her eyes.

"You see, Josie became very fond of me in the end. She liked Tom just fine as he did some chores and that for her around the farm, but Josie liked that I listened to her stories. When she went, bless her, she left us this land. One of the many properties she had gained over the years," Pearl says. "This here is my Tom."

She hands me a picture of a young man and woman and when I look closely I can see it is a younger Pearl, her shoulder wrapped in the man's arm. The man is plain looking, his skin craggily like leather which makes him look older than he probably was from time spent in the sun. He wears overalls over a plain white shirt with fields of wheat behind the couple in the background.

"Josie told me about the coins the day before she died, of course I didn't know at the time she'd left us this place," Pearl looks around the room. "I told Tom about it, and we began our own little treasure hunt."

I look down at the picture of the young couple who

probably didn't have a clue what they were getting themselves into.

"We searched this whole property it seemed a dozen times. I mean, we only had my memory of what Josie had told me to go on, something about a plant by the stream, and an old marking on a tree," Pearl shakes her head. "It wasn't much and we didn't get a stitch of luck."

"She drew a map," I say to her. "Didn't she tell you?"

Pearl lets out a laugh. "That old bat! She probably loved the thought of me and Tom circling the property till kingdom come, knowing she was smarter than the lot of us."

"So you gave up?" I ask her.

The look of sadness comes across her features again, and her eyes look down at the photo in my hand.

"Tom and I couldn't have children, you see. So this treasure hunt filled our evenings that would otherwise be spent pining away for things that would never be. One night, Tom was fixed that he thought we missed an area and kicked up a fuss about going out to look," Pearl looks away, lost in her memories. "He died in the fields before he even got to the forest. Heart attack. I found him a few hours later— when he hadn't come home I decided I needed to go out looking for him. The doctor said it was probably instant, but I still think if maybe I were with him, or if he were at home, it could have been different."

My throat tightens at the pain in her voice.

She sighs deeply before meeting my gaze again.

"Why did you want to find the treasure again after all this time?" I ask her.

The corner of her mouth lifts up.

"I don't imagine I'm going to live forever, June. And sitting here in the empty house for the past thirty years has given me a lot of time to mull everything over," she explains. "Now I've made peace with the past, but I just didn't want to go to the grave not knowing if it were all for naught."

"But why didn't you tell me about this from the beginning?" I ask her.

"Sounds silly, but I don't think Josie would have liked that," she wrinkles her nose. "It just seemed that if she wanted someone to find the coins the easy way she would have told me outright where to find 'em. You know what I mean?"

"I do," I say, and hand her back the photo.

"You keep it," she says. "You put it in that paper of yours—that historical society can't hold your granddaddy's charges over you anymore. Or, better yet, get those two old coots to make a video of you telling your story. I think Tom would have liked them, and he would have been over the moon that you found the treasure."

I nod at her and smile.

"And I want you to take the finder's fee for them coins, June," Pearl says, closing the lid of her box.

"What? No Pearl, I couldn't possibly—"

"I don't need the money," she says, shaking her head.

"With my cannabis I got more then enough to get me by. I just hope it's enough to get you by until you find that new job you're looking for.

"Pearl, that's so kind, but really I couldn't…"

"Now I won't hear another word about it," she says and straightens the end of the quilt.

I look down at the photograph of the woman smiling, a pure sense of adventure on her features.

"Thank you, Pearl," I say. "For everything."

"You know, I didn't just tell you all of that so you could write your fancy paper," she says, picking up the box off the bed.

"No?" I say, and can't help the laugh that escapes from what other possible revelation this woman could make.

"We all have dreams in the world, June," she says, looking at me. "You've got to remember that some dreams can cost you a lot more than the weight of gold to achieve, and you best be damn sure it's worth the sacrifice."

I can only nod in response as the last few days' events pass through my mind.

"But the ones that are: well, those are the ones you hold onto. They may not come true today, but for those who are willing to wait, they sure as hell will some day."

With that Pearl turns and leaves the room, the photograph of her younger self still in my hand.

Chapter Twenty-Three

I've never had to write a CV before. Biographies, sure, but not a CV. I was an intern in the Archaeology department while I did my doctorate. I was hired on there without even officially applying. All promotions came internally once someone retired or passed away, so I didn't have to apply for them either.

I look down at the blank piece of paper. The trouble is, I've only really ever had one job and I've got to fill the whole page. It's all about wording, I reason. I just have to figure out a way to mention that for my entire career I have worked at one university without having to mention that I was recently fired but all legal charges were dropped.

Naturally Oxford wasn't pleased with the YouTube video I made the day we left Colorado, outlining my discovery and Pearl's story—it's had over a million views, thank you very much. And most importantly they weren't all from the Professor and Dr Cooke pressing the bloody refresh button. Only a quarter at most. But for legal purposes I am strictly under the guise that I had no intent to release that video. I can't help that it was leaked onto the internet without my knowledge.

So far as they know at least.

Still, it's a bit of a sticky situation and I am going to take a leap and assume I shouldn't be expecting a glowing reference letter any time soon. They wouldn't even let me go and pack up my office—the contents arrived in boxes with a card yesterday. *With compliments, Phillip.*

Smug bastard.

And I can't really mention the Shield and all of that business on my CV without raising a few eyebrows. No, I'll just have to think outside of the box for this one.

Very, *very* far outside of the box.

"Griffin, where's the bloody whiskey, my lad!" I hear the Professors roar from the other side of the house.

"You're not to be drinking with your medication!" I shout before Griffin has a chance to respond.

Griffin's head pops into the doorway, and nods at the paper in front of me.

"How's it going?" he asks in an encouraging tone.

"Fine," I say, plastering a smile on my face while trying to cover the blank sheet of paper with my hands. "The rough draft is really cracking on, now."

"Well, let me know when you're done and I'll type it up for you on the typewriter," he says, smiling in return. "How's the leg?"

"Itchy," I pout, and show him the fork beside me I've been shoving inside the cast to scratch. "Only one week left now before the bloody thing's off."

"And the er… sabbatical?" he asks.

The corner of my mouth lifts briefly at the turn of phrase. That's what the Professor and him have been calling me getting sacked since we returned from America.

"Between it and this cast, I'm going a bit stir crazy to be honest," I say, looking at the boxes in the corner from my office I have yet to unpack. "I think I miss my students more than anything."

"I'm sorry, June," Griffin says, leaning on the wall. "I know that being a Professor was your life."

"No, it was my job," I say, looking up at him. "And I'm not going to just stay at a job that I don't love, that doesn't let me do the things I love, because it fits into some strange notion I have of what my life should be."

"June, don't let what I said—"

"No, you were right. And, I'd write that down because I'm not sure how often I'll be able to force myself to say it," I say, smiling up at him. "I want to start living the life that I want, not that I *should* want. And the money Pearl gave me is more than enough to get me by until I find something that fits the bill."

"And there's room for me in this new found life of yours?" he asks, tilting his head.

"It entirely revolves around you. How's your screenplay?" I ask, hoping to change the subject off me.

"Just finished the final edits," he claps his hands

together. "Got really stuck in yesterday and finished, just like you said."

"Oh, okay, well good," I say, forcing my smile wider. "Well I'd better get back to this, then we'll both be done."

I stare at him, and I have the feeling he knows I've got nothing, but he doesn't say anything. Bless him. I think we might be finally getting a hold of this relationship thing.

The doorbell chimes and he leans away from the doorframe.

"I'll get that," he volunteers.

"Be careful, it could be your Mum and Rupert, they said they may stop by," I warn him and watch as disdain washes over his features. Griffin hasn't taken to the new father figure in his life too well, and I'm not entirely sure I am encouraging him to get over it in a hurry. I'm a terrible person, I know. But between getting fired and a broken leg I've really enjoyed the peace and quiet around here lately. As soon as my leg is healed I've promised myself I'll talk Griffin round to the idea of his Mum with someone else.

Or maybe I'll just wait until after my birthday.

I make sure Griffin's gone before I lift my hands off the blank piece of paper.

I hear him open the door and a mumbled conversation before I turn my concentration back to the paper.

"June, it's for you!" Griffin yells to me.

I look up and frown. I wasn't expecting anyone.

Tucking my blank paper into the desk drawer, I get up

and gingerly make my way through the hallway on my walking cast.

"Clint," I smile as I see the young man in tight acid wash jeans on the doorstep shaking hands with Griffin. "What are you doing here?"

"I've come to see you," he says and steps to the side to reveal that he didn't come alone.

I gasp in shock and step back. "What is *he* doing here?" I ask and unconsciously grab at Griffin's sleeve to pull him back inside.

"You know who I am?" he asks, his eyebrows raised. "I guess I get around."

"Bad news travels fast," I say, straightening up.

"Sorry, who—" Griffin frowns at the man.

"Simon Locke, Daily Journal," he extends his hand to Griffin who accepts it.

"He's the one who wants the interview with the Professor," I explain to Griffin. "The one who writes all those fake letters about him winning the national lottery so he will call him."

Griffin nods in recognition.

"And you must be Griffin, I've seen your work," Simon nods.

"Yes I know, it was *"far-fetched even for British entertainment"* I believe," Griffin scowls.

Simon clears his throat, "Yes, well, loving everything doesn't sell papers, I'm afraid."

Griffin makes a non-committal sound and steps back.

"What do you want Mr Locke?" I ask. "If you want to interview the Professor, the answer is still no."

"Actually, I'm here to speak with you, Ms Jenson," he says, putting his thumbs through his suspenders.

"Me? Well, I'm not going to give your paper an interview," I say.

"June, who is it?" I hear from behind me.

I turn and close my eyes and ask the universe for strength. Of course the Professor would choose this moment to come to the door without trousers on.

"Is that my order of jelly jars?" he asks, peeking over my shoulder. "Oh Clint, it's you. How are you my lad?"

Clint blinks in shock at the Professor addressing him with his correct first name.

"I'm—I'm fine, thank you, sir," he says, nodding.

"Is it Monday? I thought we weren't meeting until Monday," he shrugs. "Never mind, will only take me a moment to locate my trousers."

"Er—it's not Monday," Clint says before the Professor turns. "I'm here to speak to June, actually."

"June?" he frowns looking from me back to Clint. "Whatever for?"

"That's where I come in," Simon says, leaning forward to rock on his toes. "I've come to propose a new project to Ms Jenson, here."

The Professor eyes him warily.

"Do you have any whiskey?" the Professor peers at the ground by Simon's feet, looking for a package.

"Er—no, no whiskey," Simon says, patting his pockets. "I have some Polos."

Simon offers the package of sweets in his outstretched hand. The Professor eyes them warily before reaching out his hand and taking the entire package.

"They'll do," he says, nodding. "Now what's this proposal for June?"

"Yes, I'd like to hear this," I say, crossing my arms across my chest.

"Well, we've seen your footage Ms Jenson—who in Britain hasn't at this point—compelling stuff I must say. We'd like to offer you a segment of your own," Simon explains.

"What kind of segment?" Griffin asks.

"Television, mainly," Simon says, which seems to perk Griffin up.

"Television?" both Griffin and I ask at the same time.

"Our newspaper is owned by a parent corporation, Globix, who produce reality television shows. We're at the beginning stages of creating a new television series, and we would like Ms Jenson here to be involved."

"What kind of television program?" I ask, and despite myself my arms relax at my sides.

"Well, I'm not sure if you are aware or not but you are quite the YouTube sensation. Clint and I have been talking—"

"Wait a minute," I interrupt. "You two know each other?"

The tops of Clint's ears turn scarlet and he has trouble meeting my eyes. "I—er—work for Mr Locke."

"You've left the Archaeological Association?" The Professor asks in confusion.

"Well, I never actually worked for them," Clint says and shoots his nervous eyes in my direction. "I work for the Daily Journal."

"You…" I frown in confusion as my mind tries to make logical sense of this. "But, what about the internship?"

"A bit of a ruse, I'm afraid," Simon Locke says and doesn't look even remotely embarrassed.

"You *lied* to them?" I say, pointing to the Professor. "So, this whole time you were following us around and recording us for your newspaper?"

At my rising voice Clint takes a tentative step back.

"How is that even *legal?*" I yell.

"Oh, we had them sign contracts. It's all on the up and up I can assure you," Simon argues.

"Up and up!" Griffin yells, shaking his head. "They don't know what day of the week it is most of the time. Did you even get them to read this contract?"

"They had a full week to review the contract. They returned it signed and sealed," Simon says.

Griffin and I turn to look at the Professor who is looking

back at us with wide eyes.

"That does sound like something I would do," he nods.

"That is so immoral, unethical," I splutter.

"I can assure you we had the best intentions," Simon says, holding his hands up in defence. "Clint here was under strict instructions to edit all footage to show an upbeat... er... *favourable* montage."

"I'm sure it was completely honourable," I say, my voice dripping with sarcasm. "Now if you are done, I think I would like you to leave."

I start to close the door on the two men, but Simon's hand comes up to block it.

"We would like you to come and host our new show. The premise is we follow you around on your adventures and see what you get up to. Of course, we have already had many historical societies reach out to us about the proposal, wanting their excavation sites to be involved. They seem thrilled to bring life back to the archaeological community," he explains, and something in his voice makes me stop.

"You've had historical societies reach out to you?" I ask, flabbergasted. "Who would possible want to work for you? You've shown yourselves to be conniving, manipulative..."

"As I said before, we had the best intentions," Simon shrugs as though this was the least problematic piece to the puzzle.

"Why are you doing this?" I ask, frowning. "You've got your story about us. What more do you want?"

Simon pauses, studying my face.

"I want more history, June."

I start to roll my eyes, but then see the earnest look on his face and pause again.

"It may be hard to believe, but I've loved history since I was a little boy. It's why I got into writing, into journalism. Believe it or not, as a little boy I didn't envision writing tatter for the Daily Journal," he laughs at himself. "When I reached out to your grandfather, it was always about the history. If you had read my letters, or let me speak to you, I could have reassured you of this. I've saved some money, and made some friends who are willing to invest in this new little adventure."

"Why should she believe anything you say?" Griffin says, shaking his head. "You've done nothing but lie to us. How do we know this isn't just another ploy to get more material on us for your gossip rag?"

Simon studies me for a moment before shrugging.

"You'll just have to take a chance I guess."

I look at the hesitant look on Griffin's face back to Simon, as the Professor offers Clint a mint.

"Well, I'm flattered I suppose, but I'm sorry, I can't do it," I say, shaking my head. "The Professor isn't well, and I couldn't ask him to put himself through it all again. He needs rest."

"Well, actually, it's you we would like Ms Jenson," he says, nodding to me. "I mean of course the others are welcome to make an appearance every now and then, but well—the public seemed to really respond to you. They think you have spunk."

"They think—" I say, and can't help the grin that tugs at my lips.

I look up at Griffin.

"Did you hear that?" I ask.

"I was standing right here," he points out.

I look back at Simon, and the smile falls.

"I can't, I'm sorry. I need to be home with my family. I can't go travelling all over the world—"

"Oh, we will be starting local," Simon says, waving away the argument. "The budget isn't going to get us to anything past Leeds right now. But we'll get there," he assures me.

"What sort of program are you looking for?" I say, narrowing my eyes in suspicion. "This isn't going to be one of those seedy programs that tries to watch me with my trousers down in the loo, is it?"

"Though the ratings suggest that's what the viewers want… No, our new production team is trying to go for a more sophisticated route on this particular project. You'd be the Alan Titchmarsh of the archaeological community."

The Professor gasps and grabs my arm.

"We love Ground Force. Watch the reruns every Thursday don't we, June Bug?" he says, and I can see the excitement on his face.

"I—" I quickly try and think it over in my head. "I don't

know. Television, it's not really anything I had considered before."

"Look, you don't have to answer right now," Simon says, reaching into his pocket and handing me a card. "You've got my number. You let me know when you make your decision."

I nod, looking down at the card.

"I must warn you not to wait too long to decide. We do have others we are considering. I believe you know a young man named Phillip—he won't bloody stop calling me…"

I take a quick intake of breath but then tell myself to calm down. I have to think about this. I'm not going to just rush into a decision because that bastard Phillip is after the same job.

The two men turn to leave just as Dr Cooke comes up the walkway.

"Clint, my lad, is it Monday?" he asks, frowning. He stops to talk to the two men for a moment as I turn and walk back into the house with the card in my hand.

"Well that was… something," Griffin says, coming to stand beside me.

I nod, not taking my eyes off of the card.

"I know. Can you believe the cheek of that man?" I ask, shaking my head. "He knowingly tricks the Professor and Dr Cooke, lies to us, and has the nerve to show up here and offer me a job."

"I know," Griffin says, clicking his tongue. "Though…"

"Though, what?" I ask him.

"Well," he says, raising his eyebrows. "It does sound like a pretty amazing opportunity."

Despite my anger, I can't help but agree. It's an offer. An offer to work on all sorts of excavation sites, running my own crew. Running my own television program. Griffin's right, it could be amazing.

I look up as Dr Cooke comes through the door.

"What was all that about?" he asks the Professor, taking off his scarf and hanging it on the rack at the front door.

"That man wants June to do a television show," the Professor says. "Daniel, do you know we weren't given that intern by the Archaeological Association? All a ruse, old chap. Some newspaper gave us Clint so they could film us. I suppose we really should have read that contract they sent..."

"Really?" Dr Cooke says, scratching his head before shrugging. "Well, that sounds like something we would do."

The Professor nods and like that the matter is settled between them. Un-bloody-believable. I definitely need to keep a closer eye on the two of them.

"And they want June to do a show with them now?" Dr Cooke asks, rubbing his chin. "I wonder if we can write it in her contract we get to keep Clint."

"And you'll never guess who we will be meeting," the Professor says in excitement.

"Dawn French," Dr Cooke guesses without hesitation.

"No," the Professor waves the guess away as though the thought was absurd. "*Alan Titchmarsh.*"

Dr Cooke gasps, his hand rising to his chest looking for some form of support. "Would he bring Charlie do you reckon?"

"Quite possible!" The Professor claps his hands together.

"Right, Professor, I'm not sure he actually mentioned you would get to meet Alan Titchmarsh," Griffin says.

"Nonsense, June will be a celebrity. We'll meet all sorts, right June?"

I nod absently, not really listening to them as I try and think this through.

"A celebrity," Dr Cooke whistles.

"Didn't ask for us, the old bugger," the Professor adjusts the elasticated band of his underpants.

"Nonsense, they're playing hard to get, Albert. I read all about this on the Internet yesterday. We've got to be a bit more savvy now we are celebrities on MyTube," Dr Cooke taps the side of his nose.

"Good thinking," the Professor says. "Did you bring whiskey, Daniel?"

"Better," Dr Cooke says, reaching into the breast pocket of his vest. "A new jelly recipe!"

The Professor's eyes light up as the two of them put their heads together over the small piece of paper.

I look to Griffin, who frowns at me.

"What?" I ask.

"You know you want to take him up on the offer," he says, studying me. "It's perfect, exactly what you want."

"Griffin, I couldn't work for that man. He's a complete snake," I argue.

"June, they're all snakes. Oxford included. Some just wear fancier suits," Griffin says.

I mull over his words before shaking my head.

"Even if I could get past the deceit, Simon said it will be local for now, but what about the future?" I ask, tilting my head in the Professor's direction. "I can't commit to something that might take me away from him. He needs me."

"That's right, he needs you," Griffin says lowering his voice so as to not be overheard by the others. "The Professor needs *you*: happy, ambitious, head-strong June who will pursue her dreams at any cost. Don't you think it would be worse for him to see you sitting around at home all day because you don't want to leave him?"

"But he said it wouldn't be local after a few months," I argue.

"Then we will come with you, and when we can't, I'll look after the Professor," he says. "Now that Mum's with Rupert she doesn't need me around as much any more."

I'm proud to say he doesn't sound nearly as hurt to make that statement as I thought he would.

"I can't ask you to do that," I say. "And what about your

writing?"

"I can write anywhere," he argues. "I'll take a break for a bit. I think I'm due, actually, with all the hours I had to put in for that screenplay."

"But, you love writing. I can't ask you to put that on hold for me–"

"Yes, you can. I love you, and I want you to be happy," he puts his arms on my waist.

"I want you to be happy too, though," I say, placing my hands on his arms.

"You being happy is the very first step to me being happy," he says, kissing the top of my forehead.

"I—I don't know," I shake my head.

"June, remember when we talked about you giving up control and not having to make all the decisions?" he asks, and I raise an eyebrow.

"Well, this is one of those times I am making the decision," he lowers his forehead to mine. "So let me."

Despite myself I laugh.

"Right, so have we decided then?" Dr Cooke asks, turning to us.

I study Griffin's face, as he looks at me in earnest.

"We have," I smile widely, looking at Griffin. "I'm taking the job."

"Right," Dr Cooke nods, turning to the Professor. "We're going to need more hats."

ABOUT THE AUTHOR

Emily Harper is the bestselling women's fiction author of White Lies, Checking Inn, My Sort-of, Kind-of Hero and the June Jenson series. Her debut novel, White Lies, was a finalist in the National Excellence in Romantic Fiction award. My Sort-of, Kind-of Hero won the RWA Book Buyer's Best award as well as the Reader's Choice award.

Originally from England, she currently lives in Canada with her family and is working on June's next adventure.

June Jenson's adventure continues in

June Jenson
and the King's Lost Treasure

Available June 2018

Chapter One

"Did you get it?" Simon Locke asks.

"Simon, I've only just come through the door." I speak into the phone held up to my ear and balance my bag, keys and the courier package precariously. "You'll have to give me a moment."

"This is top priority, June," Simon says in that upbeat, condescending tone I've come to know all too well. "Deadlines, I'm afraid. The network wants to make this their big fall production and we have to hit the ground running before someone scoops it. This is a hot commodity; I would think you would be frothing at the mouth for this."

I roll my eyes. *Everything* is a priority with the network. But that's the thing with show business that I've come to learn: it's so fast paced that things really do need to be a priority. Tomorrow it will be irrelevant.

But Simon does have a tendency to exaggerate, I reason. And lie. Like the time he had his employee, Clint, pose as the Professor and Dr Cooke's intern in order to film them and write a full exposé of our excavation in Colorado.

Now Clint seems like a part of the family. Well, a very reluctant member, but every family has to have one of those.

Travelling around the world with myself, the Professor, Dr Cooke, Griffin and myself to film the segments for *Blast from the Past*, Britain's new archaeology show, has forced Clint to become part of the fold.

"Alright, I'm opening the package now," I say, placing my bag on the foyer table and ripping open the top of the courier package. I peer inside, but there is only a single piece of paper. "You haven't given me much to go on, I see."

"I don't have much," Simon says. I can imagine him tapping his fingers on his desk, and willing me to hurry up. "The less information that is out there the better, I say. Every news station would be all over this otherwise."

I scan the paper and commit it to memory. Even if I didn't have an eidetic memory it wouldn't be hard, as there really isn't much on it.

"So, this man has just called you up, out of the blue, and wants to sell his ring?" I ask, raising my eyebrows.

"Well, he didn't call me, he called a friend of mine," Simon explains, and his lack of further explanation makes me certain this friend might not be on the up and up.

"And he thinks it is King Solomon's ring? As in the biblical king who was able to control demons with said ring?" I don't try to hide my scepticism. "Who is this man? How would he have any idea what the ring is or who it belonged to? You've just given me his address with the flimsiest description of what it looks like. It's not much to go on, is it?"

"Quite frankly, I don't want to ask him any more until we are able to get there," Simon explains. "I don't want him to fully grasp what he might have."

"Hmm… that's not very ethical," I say.

"June, he's requested ten thousand pounds in small bills. I'm not entirely sure ethics are really going to be a part of the equation here."

I frown, knowing *exactly* how I feel about that.

My head whips up at the sound of raised voices coming from upstairs.

"Listen, Simon, ethics aside, this is not a very good time," I say as the voices upstairs get louder. "The Professor is at a very tricky stage with his new medication, and I'm not sure I should uproot him right now for a wild goose chase."

"June, I understand… really, I do," he says, though his tone says otherwise. "But this isn't going to wait."

"What if I go on my own and scout it out?" I suggest.

"Not going to work, June," Simon sighs. "The viewers want to see you and the Professor *together*! We need the whole team on this one."

This makes me soften, though only slightly. Even while I was teaching at Oxford University, before I was let go for… *creative differences*, my knowledge and expertise was hardly ever sought after. Quite frankly, I got the feeling most days that my students were just there to get attendance credit. But the viewership from the show has been overwhelming. People stop us in the street to tell us how much they enjoy the program. We've even been asked for pictures and autographs.

Well, the Professor has. But, they used my pen.

"The ratings are still strong then?" I ask.

"Solid June, very solid. People can't get enough of the Professor and his faithful sidekick."

"Faithful sidekick?" I repeat, standing up straighter. I'm supposed to be the main host of the show, not the bloody sidekick.

"Yes, Dr Cooke," Simon chuckles. "What a pair they are."

I sniff, and push my black rimmed glasses further up my nose.

"Modern day Laurel and Hardy is what people are calling them," Simon says. "The video of the two of them getting chased by the ostriches in Africa... I nearly wet myself watching it."

"Well, I would hope people would be watching for the history," I say tightly.

"Oh they like that too, I'm sure," Simon says. "Anyways, I have you all scheduled for a flight Friday morning. Clint will meet you at the airport."

"Listen Simon," I say, but he interrupts.

"June, I know about the Professor, and I appreciate your predicament. But you signed on for a six episode contract to be scheduled at our discretion, and we want the both of you. You're a package deal. This is the last one before we can enter into contract renegotiations, and we need to get this done. This is the lost treasure of King Solomon we are talking about. Forget Sutton-Hoo, Cassidy's Coins—they are pittance to this discovery!"

A familiar feeling of restlessness stirs in my chest. I want to do this. If it were just me, I would already be on the plane.

But it's not just me. It hasn't been just me for a very long time.

"I'll let you know this evening," I say, and before he can respond I end the call.

Keeping the paper in my hand, I make my way up the staircase towards the Professor's bedroom. I creep up to the half open door, trying not to make a sound as I peer through the opening at the Professor's agitated face.

"I said I'm not eating that!" The Professor yells and practically throws the bowl back at Mrs Stevens. "You've put something in it."

"I bloody have not!" she yells back. "The cheek! It's the same old shite that you eat every day, nothing added, I can assure you!"

She slams the bowl down on the table next to the Professor's bed and scowls at him.

"Well, I'm not eating it!" he says, turning his nose up at the dish.

"You'll bloody well eat it, even if I have to ram it down your throat one spoon full at a time!" she bellows back at him.

I raise my eyebrows at her tone, but then straighten and remember I hired this woman for a reason. She's the only person I have ever seen the Professor cower under, and if my years of taking care of the Professor have taught me anything it's that a soft touch is ineffective. He never listened to me: not about medication, about alcohol, about driving. And he must follow the doctor's precise instructions in order for this new trial medication to work and stop his mind from deteriorating further.

A firm hand is what he needs. It's the only hope we have.

"I saw you ground those pills up and put them in the porridge when I wasn't looking," he accuses, pointing his finger at Mrs Stevens.

"If you weren't looking, how could you see a bleedin' thing?" she asks, crossing her large arms over her ample bosom. Her hair is pulled away from her face with a tattered scarf and the red splotches on her cheeks pronounce the fact she isn't wearing a stitch of makeup. I've been told she doesn't have time for that sort of nonsense. Not that I asked. She barked the information at me when I asked her if she had seen my mascara.

"I could hear you grinding them," he mutters, pulling his covers up to his neck, his blue eyes magnified behind his metal-rimmed spectacles. "It was either the pills or your massive teeth."

"I'm going to go and make a cup of tea for us," she says

in low voice, which causes the Professor to pull the blankets tighter to his chest. "And when I get back, there better not be a speck of food left in that bowl."

With that she spins on her heels and storms away from the bed. Even though I can see her coming I jump a little as she whips the door open.

"He's absolutely impossible!" she yells, before stomping passed me.

I let out the breath I wasn't aware I was holding and slowly make my way in the room. I stop just through the door and shake my head.

The Professor is propped up in bed by his pillows, glaring at the retreating back of Mrs Stevens. At the foot of the bed is Dr Cooke, also propped up by pillows. Dr Cooke joyfully spoons his own porridge into his mouth.

"Who are we, the Buckets?" I ask, my eyes shifting between Dr Cooke and the Professor. "Who should I be calling Grandpa Joe?"

"Who?" The Professor frowns.

"The family from Charlie and the Chocolate Factory have a similar set up," I gesture to the two of them.

"Do they?" the Professor asks, raising his eyebrows. "Have I met them?"

A ghost of a smile appears on my face as my heart dips a little in my chest.

"It was my favourite book as a child. You used to read it to me almost every night, remember?" I prompt. "Charlie goes to a chocolate factory when he finds the golden ticket?"

"I wouldn't mind some chocolate," the Professor muses, sitting up a little straighter and turning his attention to Dr Cooke. "Daniel?"

"Maybe some chocolate biscuits with the tea?" Dr Cooke suggests.

"You know, when I agreed to Dr Cooke coming to live with us, I wasn't aware this was going to be the arrangement," I say, raising my eyebrows.

"Oh, Daniel sleeps next door in the evenings," the Professor waves away the concern. "It's just more prudent for us to be resting in the same room during the day so Mrs Stevens doesn't have to make so many trips."

"She's not meant to be your servant!" I say, shaking my head. "She's here to give you your medicine and check up on you."

"We expanded her job description," the Professor explains. "She was too idle, and kept fussing over me with that bloody arm cuff contraption."

"That's exactly what I hired her to do," I remind him, placing my hands on my hips. "Not to make your tea and porridge."

"Which reminds me!" He peers past me to see if Mrs Stevens is out of sight and picks up the bowl of porridge he previously refused. He starts to spoon it in his mouth.

"I thought you weren't going to eat that?" I try to hide my smile.

"She loves it when I put up a fight," the Professor winks, his white hair sticking up on one side. "She fancies me."

"Mrs Stevens?" I ask, and quickly whip my head towards the door thinking she must be standing there and this is another wind up.

"Can't get enough of me. Hovers over me all day, doesn't she, Daniel?" the Professor asks, and puts another spoonful in his mouth.

"Love sick! Never leaves him alone," Dr Cooke nods, still eating his own porridge.

"Hmm, that's her job though, isn't it?" I ask, and tuck my short brown hair behind my ear.

"Beyond the call of duty, June. She's got it bad," the Professor says and places his half empty bowl back down on the table before picking up his comb. I watch as he runs it through his hair only making more of a mess of it.

"And do you—er—I mean…" I look towards the door and frown.

"You know, your grandmother wasn't a particularly attractive woman," the Professor says, taking off his glasses and using the edge of the duvet to wipe them. "I would have described her as hearty."

"You've always said I was the spitting image of her," I say, trying not to sound insulted.

The Professor ignores my comment, and put his glasses back on.

"And Mrs Stevens… Well, that woman has the thickest

ankles I've ever seen," the Professor says wistfully.

Right then.

"How are you both feeling today?" I ask as the Professor reaches for his journal and begins to write in it.

"Right as rain," he says, his eyes not leaving the paper as the pen begins to scrawl. "Though Daniel had a bit of a spell earlier."

The Professor has always kept journals, ever since he was a student at Oxford. The pages used to be filled with his daily activities, notes about historical pieces or sites he was working on.

Then his early diagnosis of Alzheimer's combined with the accusation that he stole an artefact from one of his excavation digs at Sutton-Hoo sent him into a downward spiral. His journal writing became his obsession, as he jotted down hundreds of conspiracy theories. It was only when he was exonerated from the crime that his writing returned to more simple topics.

"Are you alright?" I turn to Dr Cooke in concern.

"Yes, quite alright, thank you dear," Dr Cooke nods, but narrows his eyes at the Professor's derisive snort.

"He fainted as I was having my blood work done," the Professor explains, pointing to his journal. "Got the entire episode all down here."

"I had a diabetic attack. It was nothing to do with your blood," Dr Cooke scoffs. "I want you to change that journal entry immediately!"

The Professor pretends not to hear him.

"But you're all right now, are you?" I ask him.

"I could do with a bit more blanket," Dr Cooke says, tugging at his end and glaring at the Professor when the blanket doesn't budge.

"Is your lad back yet?" The Professor ignores him.

"Griffin's home tomorrow," I answer.

"You should have gone with him," the Professor says. "A little sun and relaxation would have done you good."

"Visiting Griffin's Mum and her new husband in Tenerife would not have been relaxing, I can assure you," I say, shaking my head.

"I'll never understand how that woman somehow convinced two men to marry her, and yet you're still unattached," the Professor says in an idle tone as he turns the page of the journal.

"Oh, thank you very much!" I say, frowning. "And I'm not *unattached*. Griffin and I live together."

"Yes, but he hasn't chiselled anything in stone, has he?" the Professor asks.

"He's testing the jam, without buying the jar," Dr Cooke agrees.

I look at the two of them and for a moment I'm speechless.

"Chiselled what? We aren't in the stone age!" I say. "Besides, maybe I don't want to get married…"

Mrs Stevens returns with the tray of tea and biscuits, and

looks at the half empty porridge bowl beside the Professor but makes no comment.

"Keep this up any longer and you'll end up a spinster, June," the Professor says and flicks his eyes in the direction of Mrs Stevens. "Such a waste."

Unsure now as to whether he is referring to me or the well-endowed Mrs Stevens, I purse my lips.

"Not that I am a spinster, but there is nothing wrong with not getting married," I argue. I ignore the slight twinge in my chest as I say this. "It's a new day and age… And besides, I would hardly have time while looking after you two. Apparently you're too ill to even get up!"

I'm not even sure marriage is something that's important to me. I've always had greater focuses in my life. Like the Professor, and my career.

And yes, now that the Professor is getting older and he has Dr Cooke and Mrs Stevens I'm not needed as much, but that doesn't mean I'm not needed at all.

And yes, my career has taken a drastic turn in the last year, which gives me much more time to myself. But I fill that time with important things. Like reading, and writing, and… er… gardening.

Well I just trimmed the hedge in the front yard, but it's something, isn't it?

"Maybe you are sending your young lad the wrong signals," Mrs Stevens suggests as she hands the Professor and Dr Cooke their cups of tea, before handing me the last cup on the tray.

"What 'signal' is that?" I ask her before I can stop myself. Honestly, this is absolutely ridiculous. I'm not sure how we even got onto this topic. I don't want to get married. Well, I don't *need* to get married.

"Well, is that how you've always done your hair?" she asks me.

"Er—yes…" I say, bringing my hand to my chin length, wavy brown hair.

What's wrong with my hair?

"Oh, alright. It can't be that, then. I didn't know if you made a bit more of an effort with it when you were first together."

"More of an…" I bluster. "What is *that* supposed to mean?"

"Maybe it's the glasses," Dr Cooke chimes in.

"What's wrong with my glasses?" I ask, and instinctively push them further up my nose.

"Oh, they're fine," Dr Cooke replies quickly. "I only meant they draw attention to the fact you don't really do much to your face. I've always thought you looked lovely with a little rouge."

I open my mouth to retort, but the Professor speaks before I get a chance.

"June's face is fine," he says, patting my hand and I soften. "It's those clothes and that god awful bag she's always carting around that are the real issue."

"I—" I straighten my back and remove my hand from his. "I love that bloody bag and you know it!"

I look down at my clothes, and honestly, they're not *that* bad. A nice clean pair of trousers and a button down blouse, tucked in. Practical and classic, I assure myself. I've never been one for patterns or prints. For the majority of my adult life I lived under a cloud of suspicion when the Professor was accused of stealing the priceless relic from Sutton-Hoo. I did everything possible to avoid any attention, and that included modest dress. And since he was acquitted of the scandal a few years ago—well, old habits die hard, I'm afraid.

Also, these trousers happen to be very comfortable.

And my bag. My brown leather knapsack has seen me through so much, it has been everywhere with me.

I'm rather quite attached to that bag.

"As I've always said, June Bug, never ask questions you don't want the answers to," the Professor tells me.

"I never asked!" I argue, and take a deep breath, attempting to calm myself down. "Besides, I happen to have a very fulfilling life, and I don't need to get married."

"See, now there's the spirit," Mrs Stevens collects the tray with the dirty dishes before making her way to the bedroom door. "Then you won't be disappointed when no one asks."

I choke on some of my tea and it dribbles down my chin.

"God I love to watch that woman waddle," the Professor says, peering past me to the now empty doorway.

"Listen, as much as I love hearing about my doomed marital status, I did come in here for a purpose," I say, resting my cup of tea on my knee.

"Oh?" the Professor says, reaching for his journal once again.

"Have the new jam jars arrived?" Dr Cooke asks, his eyes lighting up.

"Er—I'm not sure," I say, shaking my head. "I've had a call from Simon."

"Oh," Dr Cooke sighs, deflated, while the Professor continues to read something he just wrote in his journal.

The two of them used to be so eager for a glimpse of adventure and now they barely want to leave their bed.

"Yes, well, he's sent this," I say, handing the paper in my hand to Dr Cooke. "It seems a very interesting project."

Dr Cooke scans the page and snorts.

"The lost treasure of King Solomon?" He shakes his head and hands the paper to the Professor. "It hasn't been seen or heard of in centuries."

I turn to look at the Professor as he studies the sheet.

"Well?" I prompt.

"They have nothing," he says, putting the paper down beside him and reaching again for his journal. "They've found someone who is attempting to sell a gold ring on the black market. It could be anything. It could be nothing. Probably out to make a quick few."

My shoulders sink at his words.

"But… But you don't *know* that it is nothing!" I argue.

"That paper says that the description of the ring *could* potentially be something related to King Solomon because of the markings—it could be *anything*. A copy, another ring from the same era, a forgery…" he argues right back.

"Yes, but… it could *not* be. Don't you—don't you want to *know?*" I look at the two of them perplexed. It's like I am not looking at the same two men who my whole life have carted me off on a thousand wild goose chases, in the hopes that maybe, just once it wouldn't be.

The Professor just shrugs.

"I—I can't believe this!" I yell at them both. "This is the lost treasure of King Solomon I am talking about and the two of you are sitting there like you can't be bothered."

Dr Cooke sighs. "June, archaeology is a young man's game—"

"No, it's not!" I interrupt. "It's a dying art, for exactly the opposite reason."

"It's a lot to constantly get on a plane," Dr Cooke sulks. "Can't they just send the picture of the ring here? Why do we need to go all the way to Cairo?"

"I don't believe what I'm hearing…" I shake my head. "I can't believe I am standing here, trying to convince you two to come on an adventure with me."

"You're always telling me I'm too unwell to do things; I'm finally agreeing with you," the Professor points out.

"Yes, but that's what we *do*, isn't it?" I ask, throwing my arms up in the air. "You say you want to come. I say you can't because its too dangerous, and then you weasel your way into coming somehow anyways!"

"Weasel?" the Professor sits up straighter. "Listening to you someone may think we somehow intrude on your life."

Both look affronted.

"You do!" I say to them. "But that's half the fun, isn't it?"

"Well, we won't *intrude* this time, will we, Daniel?" the Professor says.

"Certainly not," Dr Cooke agrees tersely.

"That's not what I meant and you know it. I just can't believe the two of you want this," I gesture at the bed and the teacups, "to be the rest of your lives."

"I'm tired," the Professor says, crossing his arms across his chest. "She's taken away my bloody whiskey and put me on a gluttonous diet!"

"It's a gluten-free diet," I correct him.

"She's taken away my jam," he sulks.

"If you come with me, you can have jam and scones for breakfast every day," I coax.

He studies me for a minute before sighing.

"What's the point?" he asks. "She'll only take them away when I get back."

"This doesn't sound like you," I frown. "You're usually the first one out of the door when something exciting comes along."

"My knees hurt," he waves his hand to the end of the bed.

"I'll get you braces," I say.

"And they don't make my tea right in foreign countries," he argues.

"So, what?" I ask, shaking my head. "You're just giving up?"

"It's called retirement," the Professor says. "And we find it suits us well."

Retirement? I'm not sure that's a word I have ever heard out of his mouth before.

"And you agree with him?" I ask Dr Cooke.

"Well…" he starts.

"Daniel is retiring too. We are going to rest now and make jam," the Professor interrupts. "Well, I'll make it and he'll eat it. Unless she bloody takes it off him as well."

"What's all the shouting about?" Mrs Stevens says from behind me, and I jump at her voice.

"I—," I hesitate at her intimidating stare but continue. "I was trying to convince these two to come to Egypt with me to have a look at a ring."

"Never buy your own engagement ring, dear," Mrs Stevens pats my shoulder. "It sends a very *needy* message. He'll ask you one day, I'm sure."

"Not a ring for me," I say through gritted teeth. "It's potentially an important historical relic, and I want these two to come with me to validate the piece."

"Oh," she nods. "Well, in that case, absolutely not. He's in too fragile of a state. I've only just got his blood pressure back under control."

"Of course I would never dream of doing it if I thought it would be detrimental to the Professor's health," I say, feeling the need to defend myself. "I would closely monitor him at all times, and you are welcome to come with us as well if you think it would help."

"I can't fly; I've got a bad hernia." She points to a small bulge in her shirt.

"Oh good God," I say, before I catch myself. "Er—the network will also be providing medical care for the Professor in Cairo should he need it."

"It won't do," she says shaking her head. "I'm afraid the answer is no."

"No?" I say, raising one eyebrow. "I'm sorry, I didn't know that this was your decision to make."

"He's *my* patient," she says, straightening her back and staring at me.

"And he's *my* grandfather," I say, straightening my own to try and match her intimidating height.

"If anyone is at all concerned, I also don't think I should go," Dr Cooke raises his arm from the bed.

"When's the last time you two left this room?" I ask, looking around at the stacked books and piles of papers.

"Daniel and I had tea in the garden with you yesterday," the Professor waves his hand.

"That was two weeks ago," I argue, looking up at Mrs Stevens, who has her hands on her hips. "He should be getting up and about."

"He needs to stay comfortable." She narrows her eyes at me. "It's the best thing for him."

"Says who?" I ask her.

"He's gone four days without a single episode," she says, lifting her chin in pride.

"Because he hasn't been able to do anything to forget," I argue, turning to look back at the Professor. "You shouldn't stay cooped up like this."

"I'm fine," he says, patting my hand before reaching for his pen again. "Besides Karen has just taken Mitch back on Eastenders."

"This is ridiculous," I say to him. "Yes, you have to take your medication and scale back a bit, but you still have to live your life."

"You know, I am a certified healthcare practitioner," Mrs Stevens says, and swoops in front of me to check the Professor's temperature. "I think I know what I am doing."

"He doesn't have a fever, he's fine!" I shake my head.

"I think I will decide that," she says, taking the thermometer out of the Professor's mouth and studying it. "Hmm…"

"I think I'd like mine checked as well," Dr Cooke says, putting the back of his hand to his forehead.

"Oh for God's sake, you're both fine!" I shout at them.

"Don't you want him to be as comfortable as possible?" Mrs Stevens asks me. "I mean, I was under the impression that this was the reason for me being here."

"Of course I do," I say. "But I still want him to be... *him*."

"I think it is time you face the reality of the situation," Mrs Stevens says to me, shaking the thermometer in my direction. "These men are not young anymore. They need proper care and rest."

"Well, they're certainly not going to sit here in bed and waste away," I say to her, my hands on my hips. "I appreciate everything you are doing for my grandfather, I really do. But he is an archaeologist. He belongs in the field, discovering history, with me."

"You're living in the past, girl," Mrs Stevens shakes her head. "Some days he doesn't even know who he is. Do you want to make that worse by dragging him out on some cockamamie adventure that could turn out to be nothing?"

"But it could turn out to be everything!" I retort, and turn to the Professor. "It's the lost treasure of *King Solomon*. This would be one of the greatest discoveries the world has ever seen! I just cannot allow you to not want to be a part of it."

And suddenly it is very important for him to understand. This isn't about me, or him. This is about history. Some of the most important history this world will ever know, and that's not something I would have ever imagined him to turn down.

"If I didn't think you could do this, I would have already told the network no," I say to him.

The Professor looks from Mrs Stevens glaring face to my beseeching one.

"We can do this," I say to him.

"I don't know, June," the Professor sighs, shaking his head.

I gulp down the panic that rises in my chest. This is my new worry in life, and I realize it is a full turnaround. Before it was whether he was going to take his trousers off in public, or whether he would find the key to the liquor cabinet. But no, it is this complete lack of energy, of will, that now has me absolutely heartbroken. Before I felt a fighting chance, but this acceptance of his circumstance and life is terrifying to me.

And it just won't do.

"One more adventure," I say to him, putting my hand on his knee.

He looks at me earnestly and we study each other.

The lines around his eyes are becoming increasingly deep, magnified by the silver rimmed spectacles that sit on the bridge of his nose. But his bright blue eyes are still lively and I can see a hint of excitement in them, whether he wants to acknowledge it or not. He's still there: my grandfather. The man who has dedicated his life to the discovery and preservation of our world's history.

And I realize that I don't care what it takes, or what I have to do—this is what makes my grandfather the man who he is, and I will protect that with whatever power I have in this world. And until that light extinguishes in his eyes, I'll know I have not have fully lost him.

"One more adventure," the Professor tests the words.

"I want it on record that I thoroughly disputed this decision!" Mrs Stevens sniffs from behind me.

"Noted," I nod, still smiling at the Professor.

"Daniel?" he raises his eyebrow at Dr Cooke.

"Oh, alright," Dr Cooke sighs, pulling the blanket further up his chest. "But I'm not bloody sitting in coach!"